A TALE DARK & GRIMM

New Delhi Hong Kong • SCHOLASTIC INC. • New York Toronto London Auckland Sydney Mexico City

A TALE DARK & GRIMM

ADAM GIDWITZ

ISBN 978-0-545-42528-5

Copyright © 2010 by Adam Gidwitz.
All rights reserved. Published by Scholastic Inc., 557 Broadway,
New York, NY 10012, by arrangement with Dutton Children's Books,
a division of Penguin Young Readers Group, a member of
Penguin Group (USA) Inc. SCHOLASTIC and associated logos
are trademarks and/or registered trademarks of Scholastic Inc.

12 11 10 9 8 7 6 5 4 3 2 1   11 12 13 14 15 16/0

Printed in the U.S.A.   23

This edition first printing, September 2011

Designed by Irene Vandervoort

To my family. Obviously.

Contents

*O*nce upon a time, fairy tales were awesome.

I know, I know. You don't believe me. I don't blame you. A little while ago, I wouldn't have believed it myself. Little girls in red caps skipping around the forest? Awesome? I don't think so.

But then I started to read them. The real, Grimm ones. Very few little girls in red caps in those.

Well, there's one. But she gets eaten.

"Okay," you're probably saying, "if fairy tales are awesome, why are all the ones I've heard so unbelievably, mind-numbingly boring?" You know how it is with stories. Someone tells a story. Then somebody repeats it and it changes. Someone else repeats it, and it changes again. Then someone's telling it to their kid and taking out all the scary, bloody scenes—in other words, the awesome parts—and the next thing you know the story's about an adorable little girl in a red cap, skipping through the forest to take cookies to her granny. And you're so bored you've passed out on the floor.

The real Grimm stories are not like that.

Take *Hansel and Gretel*, for example. Two greedy little children try to eat a witch's house, so she decides to cook and eat them instead—which is fair, it seems to me. But before she can follow through on her (perfectly reasonable) plan, they lock her in an oven and bake her to death.

Which is pretty cool, you have to admit.

But maybe it's not awesome.

Except—and here's the thing—that's not the real story of Hansel and Gretel.

You see, there is another story in Grimm's *Fairy Tales*. A story that winds all throughout that moldy, mysterious tome—like a trail of bread crumbs winding through a forest. It appears in tales you may never have heard, like *Faithful Johannes* and

Brother and Sister. And in some that you have—*Hansel and Gretel,* for instance.

It is the story of two children—a girl named Gretel and a boy named Hansel—traveling through a magical and terrifying world. It is the story of two children striving, and failing, and then not failing. It is the story of two children finding out the meanings of things.

Before I go on, a word of warning: Grimm's stories—the ones that weren't changed for little kids—are violent and bloody. And what you're going to hear now, the one true tale in *The Tales of Grimm,* is as violent and bloody as you can imagine.

Really.

So if such things bother you, we should probably stop right now.

You see, the land of Grimm can be a harrowing place. But it is worth exploring. For, in life, it is in the darkest zones one finds the brightest beauty and the most luminous wisdom.

And, of course, the most blood.

A Tale Dark & Grimm

Faithful
Johannes

*O*nce upon a time, in a kingdom called Grimm, an old king lay on his deathbed. He was Hansel and Gretel's grandfather—but he didn't know that, for neither Hansel nor Gretel had been born yet.

Now hold on a minute.

I know what you're thinking.

I am well aware that nobody wants to hear a story that happens *before* the main characters show up. Stories like that are boring, because they all end exactly the same way. With the main characters showing up.

But don't worry. This story is like no story you've ever heard.

You see, Hansel and Gretel don't just *show up* at the end of this story.

They show up.

And then they get their heads cut off.

Just thought you'd like to know.

The old king knew he was soon to pass from this world, and so he called for his oldest and most faithful servant. The servant's name was Johannes; but he had served the king's father, and his father's father, and his father's father's father so loyally that all called him Faithful Johannes.

Johannes tottered in on bowed legs, heaving his crooked back step by step and leering with his one good eye. His long nose sniffed at the air. His mouth puckered around two rotten teeth. But, despite his grotesque appearance, when he came within view, the old king smiled and said, "Ah, Johannes!" and drew him near.

The king's voice was weak as he said, "I am soon to die. But before I go, you must promise me two things. First, promise that you will be as faithful to my young son as you have been to me."

Without hesitation, Johannes promised.

The old king went on. "Second, promise that you will show him his entire inheritance—the castle, the treasures, all this fine land—*except* for one room. Do not show him the room with the portrait of the golden princess. For if he sees the portrait he will fall madly in love with her. And I fear it will cost him his life."

The king gripped Johannes's hand. "Promise me."

Again Johannes promised. Then the wrinkles of worry left the king's brow, and he closed his eyes and breathed his last.

Soon the prince was crowned as the new king. He was celebrated with parades and toasts and feasts all throughout the kingdom. But, when the revelry finally abated, Johannes sat him down for a talk.

First, Johannes described to him all of the responsibilities of the throne. The young king tried not to fall asleep.

Then he explained that the old king had asked him to show the young king his entire inheritance—the castle, the treasures, all this fine land. At the word *treasures* the young king's face lit up. Not that he was greedy. It was just that he found the idea of treasures exciting.

Finally, Johannes tried to explain his own role to the young king. "I have served your father, and your father's father, and your father's father's father before that," Johannes said. The young king started calculating on his fingers how that was even possible, but before he could get very far, Johannes had moved on. "They call me Faithful Johannes because I have devoted my life to the Kings of Grimm. To helping them. To advising them. To under-standing them."

"Understanding them?" the young king asked.

"No. Under-standing them. In the ancient sense of the word. Standing beneath them. Supporting them. Bearing their troubles and their pains on my shoulders."

The young king thought about this. "So you will under-stand me, too?" he asked.

"I will."

"No matter what?"

"Under any circumstances. That is what being faithful means."

"Well, under-stand that I am tired of this, and would like to see the treasures now." And the young king stood up.

Faithful Johannes shook his head and sighed.

They began by exploring every inch of the castle—the treasure crypts, the towers, and every single room. Every single room, that is, save one. One room remained locked, no matter how many times they passed it.

Well, the young king was no fool. He noticed this. And so he asked, "Why is it, Johannes, that you show me every room in the palace, but never *this* room?"

Johannes squinted his one good eye and curled up his puckered, two-toothed mouth. Then he said, "Your father asked me not to show you that room, Your Highness. He feared it might cost you your life."

I'm sorry, I need to stop for a moment. I don't know what you're thinking right now, but when I first heard this part of the story, I thought, "What, is he crazy?"

Maybe you know something about young people, and maybe you don't. I, having been one myself once upon a time, know a few things about them. One thing I know is that if you don't want one to do something—for example, go into a room where there's a portrait of an unbearably beautiful princess—saying "It might cost you your life" is about the *worst* thing you could possibly say. Because then that's *all* that young person will want to do.

I mean, why didn't Johannes say something else? Like, "It's a broom closet. Why? You want to see a broom closet?" Or, "It's a fake door, silly. For decoration." Or even, "It's the ladies' bathroom, Your Majesty. Best not go poking your head in there."

Any of those would have been perfectly sufficient, as far as I can tell.

But he didn't say any of those things. If he had, none of the horrible, bloody events to follow would ever have happened.

(Well, in that case, I guess I'm glad he told the truth.)

"Cost me my life?!" the young king proclaimed with a toss of his head. "Nonsense!" He insisted he be let into the room. First he demanded. But Johannes refused. Then he commanded. Still Johannes refused. Then he threw himself on the floor and had a fit, which was very unbecoming for a young man the king's age. Finally, Faithful Johannes realized there was little he could do. So, wrinkling his old, malformed face into a wince, he unlocked and opened the door.

The king burst into the room. He found himself staring, face-to-face with the most beautiful portrait of the most beautiful woman he had ever seen in his life. Her hair looked like it was spun from pure gold thread. Her eyes flashed like the ocean on a sunny day. And yet, around her lips, there was a hint of sadness, of loneliness.

The young king took one look at her and fainted dead away.

———

Later, in his room, he came to. Johannes hovered over his bed. "Who was that radiant creature?" the king asked.

"That, Your Majesty, is the golden princess," Johannes answered.

"She's the most beautiful woman in the world," the young king said.

And Johannes answered, "Yes, she is."

"And yet she looked almost sad. Why is that?"

Johannes took a deep breath, and replied, "Because, young king, she is cursed. Every time she has tried to marry, her husband has died; and it is said that a fate worse than death is destined for her children, if ever she should have any. She lives in a black marble palace, topped with a golden roof, all by herself. And, as you can imagine, she is terribly lonely and terribly sad."

The king sat straight up in his bed and grabbed the front of Faithful Johannes's tunic. And though he stared into the old man's face, he saw only the princess's ocean-bright eyes and her lips ringed with sadness. "I must have her," he said. "I will marry her. I will save her."

"You may not survive," Johannes said.

"I will survive, if you help me. If you are faithful to me, if you under-stand me, you'll do it."

Johannes feared for the young king's life. But he had under-stood the young king's father, and his father's father, and his father's father's father before that. What could he say?

Johannes sighed. "I'll do it."

It was widely known that in all the golden princess's days of loneliness, the only thing that gave her any modicum of happiness was gold. So Johannes told the king to gather all of the gold in the kingdom and to command his goldsmiths to craft the most exquisite golden objects that the world had ever seen. Which soon was done.

Then Johannes disguised himself and the king as merchants and loaded a ship with the golden goods. And they set off for the land of the golden princess.

As their ship's prow split the sea, Johannes tutored the king in his part: "You're a gold merchant, Your Majesty. The princess has always loved gold, but these days, it is the only thing that gives her any joy. So when I bring her to the ship, charm her not only with your gentle manners and fine looks, but also with the gold. Then, perhaps, she will be yours."

When they landed, the king readied the ship and tended to his merchant costume, while Johannes, carrying a few golden objects in his bag, made his way to the towering ramparts of black marble where the golden princess lived. He entered the courtyard, and there discovered a serving girl retrieving water from a well with a golden bucket.

"Pretty maid," he said, smiling his kind but unhandsome smile, "do you think your lady might be interested in such trifling works of gold as these?" And he produced two of the finest, most exquisite golden statuettes that man's hand has ever made.

The girl was stunned by their beauty. She took them from Johannes and hurried within. Not ten minutes had elapsed before the golden princess herself emerged from the castle, holding the statuettes in her hands. She was as gorgeous as her portrait—more so in fact—and as she greeted Johannes, her golden hair flashed in the light and her ocean-blue eyes danced with pleasure. Still, around her lips there was sadness.

"Tell me, old man," she said, "are these really for sale? I've never seen anything so beautiful, so fine."

Faithful Johannes bowed. "But there is more, fair princess, much more. My master's ship is full of such wonders. And they can be yours, if you will just accompany me down to the harbor."

The princess hesitated for a moment—since her last husband-to-be had died, she had not set foot outside the palace. But the allure of the gold was too strong. She threw a shining traveling cloak over her shoulders and followed Johannes to the boat.

The young king, in his disguise as a merchant, greeted her.

Her beauty was so stunning, her sadness so apparent and so tender, that he nearly fainted again. But somehow he did not, and she smiled at him and invited him to show her all the treasures he had brought to her fair land.

As soon as they had descended below the deck, Johannes hurried to the captain of the ship, and, in whispered tones, instructed him to cast off from shore and set sail for home immediately.

Now, my young readers, I know just what you're thinking. You're thinking, *Hmmm. Stealing a girl. That's an* interesting *way of winning her heart.* Allow me to warn you now that, under any other circumstances, stealing a girl is about the worst way of winning her heart you could possibly cook up.

But, because this happened long ago, in a faraway land, it seems to have worked.

For the golden princess came back up to the deck and saw that her land was far away from her. At first she did indeed protest, and fiercely, too, that she'd been carried away by lowborn merchants. But when one of the "merchants" revealed himself to be a king, and revealed that, in addition, he was madly in love with her, and when, besides, Johannes assured her that, if she *really* wanted to, she could go home, but she couldn't take the gold if she did, the princess realized that in fact the young king was just the kind of man she would like to marry after all, and decided that she'd give the whole matrimony thing one last shot.

And they all lived happily ever after.

The End

Are there any small children in the room? If so, it would be best if we just let them think this really is the end of the story and hurried them off to bed. Because this is where things start to get, well . . . awesome.

But in a horrible, bloody kind of way.

As the ship plowed through the purple sea, the new lovers made moon-faces at each other up near the bow. Faithful Johannes was sitting near the back of the ship, admiring the success of his plan, when he noticed three ravens alight on a mast beam.

The first raven motioned with his beak at the king and princess. "What a lovely couple those two make," he said.

And the second said, "Yes. Too bad they won't stay that way."

The first said, "What do you mean?"

"Well," the second replied, "when the ship gets to land, a beautiful chestnut stallion will canter up to the group, and the king will decide to ride it back to the castle. But if he does, he will be thrown from its back and die."

"Good God, that's horrible!" said the first raven. "Is there nothing anyone can do?"

"Oh, there is," said the second raven. "Someone could kill the horse before the king mounts it. But what good is that? For

ADAM GIDWITZ

if someone did it, and told *why* he did it, he would be turned to stone, from the tips of his toes to the knobs of his knees."

"To stone?" asked the first raven.

"To stone," answered the second.

The third raven, who'd been listening quietly, cut in at this point. "It gets worse, you know," he said. "If, by some chance, the two lovers escape that danger, another lies ahead. For when they arrive at the gates of the castle, a beautiful bridal gown, made of pure gold, will be laid out on a bed of purple flowers. The princess will want to wear it, of course. But if she touches it she will be consumed by a ball of fire and burn to a cinder right there on the spot."

"Good God, that's terrible!" cried the first raven. "Is there nothing anyone can do?"

"Oh, there is," said the third raven. "If someone were to pick up the dress before she could, and throw it in the fire, the princess would live. But what good is that? For if someone did it, and told *why* he did it, he would be turned to stone, from the knobs of his knees to the core of his heart."

"To stone?" repeated the first raven.

"To stone," confirmed the third.

"Nor is that all," said the second raven morosely. "For if the two lovers avoid that tragedy, a final one awaits. When they are married and begin the wedding dance, the new queen will swoon, and fall to the floor, and die."

"Good God, that's the worst thing yet!" cried the first raven. "Is there nothing anyone can do?"

"Oh, there is," said the third. "If someone were to bite the new queen's lip and suck three drops of blood from it with his mouth, she would live. But what good is that? For if someone did it, and told *why* he did it, he would be turned to stone from the core of his heart to the top of his head."

"To stone?" said the first.

"To stone," replied the second.

"To stone," echoed the third.

And with that, the three ravens shook their black beaks, sighed sadly, and flew away.

Faithful Johannes buried his head in his hands, for he had heard all. He knew what he would have to do, and that it could not come to good.

Just as the ravens had foretold, after the ship landed and the king and his wife-to-be had been greeted by all the servants and courtiers of the castle, a beautiful chestnut stallion cantered up to the group. The king, taken with the beast's beauty, announced that it would bear him in triumph back to the castle. But before

ADAM GIDWITZ

he could mount it, Johannes slipped onto its back, drew a blade, and cut the horse's throat, soaking its silken coat with warm, red blood. It collapsed to the ground in a heap.

Cries of shock went up from the crowd. The other servants, who had never loved misshapen Johannes, whispered, "To kill the king's new stallion! Treason! Treason!"

The king looked back and forth between Johannes and the dead horse. Johannes's face had no expression. At last, the young king said, "Johannes was faithful to my father and to my father's father and to my father's father's father before that. He has always under-stood us. So I will under-stand him. If he does it, it must be right."

Not another word was said about the subject, and the party proceeded, afoot, back to the palace.

When they arrived at the gate they saw a beautiful golden bridal gown, lying on a bed of purple roses.

"Oh! I shall wear it in the wedding!" the queen-to-be exclaimed, running to take hold of the marvelous garment.

But before she could reach it, Johannes grabbed it from the flower bed and strode into the great hall, where he threw it into the fire.

Again, the party was taken with cries of shock and dismay. The servants huddled together and whispered, "Treason! Treason!"

But the king hushed them. "Johannes has always been faithful to me and my family. So I will be faithful to him. If he does it, it must be right."

The young king and golden princess were married the very next day. The princess looked particularly beautiful, her ocean-blue eyes brimming with joy. But Johannes watched anxiously.

They moved to dance, and the music began. But they had not taken two steps when the new queen suddenly swooned and fell to the ground. Before anyone else could move, Johannes swept in, lifted her to his chest, and carried her out of the hall.

He hurried through empty hallways, carrying the new queen in his arms, to a narrow, winding staircase that led to the highest turret in the castle—his private chamber. When they arrived, he placed her carefully on the floor, bent over her, and, with his two rotten teeth, bit her lip until he drew blood. Then, ever so tenderly, the unhandsome man sucked three drops of blood from her lip with his mouth.

The queen began to stir. But just then, the king burst into the room. He had followed Johannes all through the palace and had watched at a crack in the door as Johannes—his once faithful Johannes—had done something unspeakable to his new queen.

ADAM GIDWITZ

"Treason!" he bellowed at the top of his lungs. "Treason!" The other servants quickly ran to their king's aid.

"King!" Johannes said. "Please! Trust me!"

"Take him to the dungeons!" the young king shouted. "Tomorrow, he dies!"

The next day, Johannes was led from the dungeons to the top of a funeral pyre. There he was tied as a torch was readied to set the great stack of hay and tinder on fire.

The king watched with his new queen at his side. She had fully recovered from the day before. But both wore black, and their faces were somber. "He was like a father to me," the young king said. The queen took his hand.

The executioner lit his torch and brought it to the pyre, its sparks leaping eagerly at the dry tinder. Behind the king, the jealous servants muttered and smiled to one another.

But just before the executioner could set the pyre alight, Johannes called out, "King! To whom I have been faithful, and to whose father, and father's father, and father's father's father I was faithful before that. Will you allow me to speak before I die?"

The young king sadly inclined his head and said, "Speak."

And so Johannes spoke. He told of seeing the three ravens on the ship. He told of hearing them speak. He told of their prophecy of the chestnut stallion.

And as he told it, he turned to stone, from the tips of his toes to the knobs of his knees.

All the spectators gasped. But Johannes went on.

He told of the ravens' prophecy of the bridal gown.

And as did, he turned to stone, from the knobs of his knees to the core of his heart.

In the crowd, mouths fell open.

Finally, he told of the ravens' prophecy of the wedding dance.

And when he had, he turned to stone, from the core of his heart to the top of his head.

And he died.

A great wail went up from all assembled. For they had learned, too late, that Johannes had been faithful to the very end, and had given his life for his king.

The king and the queen, in an effort to honor his memory, took Faithful Johannes, grotesque even in stone, and placed him beside their bed so that every morning when they woke up, and every evening when they lay down, they would be reminded of his faithfulness, and the great debt they owed him.

The End

Well, not really.

More like, The Beginning. For it is here that the tale of Hansel and Gretel truly begins.

The king and the queen soon had a pair of beautiful twins, a girl and a boy. They named the boy Hansel and the girl Gretel. They were the light of their parents' lives. Hansel was dark like his father, with black curly hair and charcoal eyes. Gretel was fair like her mother, with hair that looked like it was spun from pure gold thread and eyes that shone like the sea. They were happy children, full of play and mischief and joy. So happy were they, in fact, that they nearly made their parents forget the faithful servant who had saved their lives, and how they had betrayed him.

Nearly. But not quite.

And one day, as the king played with Hansel and Gretel at the foot of his bed, and the queen was off in chapel praying, he began to cry. "He under-stood me," the king said, "though I did not under-stand him." He fell to the foot of the statue and wept. When his tears touched the stone, something miraculous happened. Johannes spoke.

"There is a way, king," the stone Johannes said, "to rescue me from this rock, if you truly wish it."

"Oh, I do!" the king cried. "I'll do anything! Anything!"

And Johannes said . . .

There are no young children in the room, right? You're certain? Okay . . .

And Johannes said, "You must cut off the heads of your children, and smear my statue with their blood. And then, and only then, will I return to life."

Remember what I told you would happen when Hansel and Gretel finally showed up?

The king collapsed on the bed, weeping. But he felt he had no choice. "You under-stood me always, no matter what," he said. "So I will under-stand you." He stood, beckoned Hansel and Gretel to his side, drew a sword from its place on the wall, and cut off their heads. Their lifeless bodies dropped to the floor.

———

See?

ADAM GIDWITZ

The king took their blood on his hands and smeared it on the statue. Just as he had foretold, Johannes returned to life, covered in the children's blood. And the king, despite the blood, and through his tears at his own children's deaths, threw his arms around his faithful servant, Johannes.

The End

Nearly.

Johannes smiled his sweet, crooked smile and said, "You have under-stood me, at the greatest cost." And he placed little Hansel's head back on his body, and little Gretel's head on hers, and instantly they began to leap and play as if nothing had happened, and as if they were not covered in blood. And the king threw his arms around them, and then again around Johannes, and they all laughed with joy.

The End

Almost.

For just then, the king heard the queen's footsteps echoing in the hall. He looked at Johannes, back from the dead, and their children, covered in blood. "Quickly!" he said, and hurried them all into a wardrobe.

When the queen came into the room, he asked her how her prayers had gone. And she replied, "I can barely pray. I think only of Johannes, and how we failed him."

And the king replied, "What if I told you, dear queen, that there was a way to repay our debt to Johannes, and to bring him back to life, but that it was a terrible way, and it would cost us everything that is most dear to us. What would you say?"

"Anything!" the queen cried. "Anything we can do, we must do! We owe it to him!"

"Even if it meant killing our two children?" the king asked.

The queen gasped. She fell to the floor and wept bitterly. At last she said, "I would never do it. I could never do it. But I know we should. We owe him our lives."

"I couldn't agree more!" the king exclaimed. "And that's why . . . " As he said this, he opened the wardrobe doors, and out came their two beloved children, all covered in blood, followed by a living, breathing Johannes. The queen screamed and fainted. The king threw a basin of water in her face, and she woke up and screamed again. Then the king explained it all to her, and she wept and laughed and threw her arms first around her children and after around Johannes, and then she held them all at once and wept and laughed some more.

The End

Sort of.

You see, the way the Brothers Grimm tell it, that is the end. But it isn't really. Not at all.

For as the king recounted what had happened to his wife, Hansel and Gretel heard. And understood.

Late that night, they lay in their beds, unable to sleep.

"Hansel," Gretel said.

"Yes, Gretel?"

"Did you hear what Father said?"

"Yes."

"He cut off our heads to save that ugly old man."

Hansel was silent.

"And Mommy was glad that he did. Do you think they hate us?"

Hansel was silent still.

"I think we should run away," Gretel said. "In case they want to do it again."

"That's just what I was thinking," Hansel answered. "Just what I was thinking. . . ."

Hansel
and Gretel

*O*nce upon a time, two children left their home and walked out into the wide, wild world.

The land was dark as Hansel and Gretel made their way across the level turf beyond the palace moat. They had never left the palace by themselves before, and they knew little of the great world beyond its walls. But they had been frightened by what their father had done. And they believed firmly in their little hearts that parents should not kill their children, and they were resolved to punish theirs by going out and finding a family that was as nice as a family should be.

How to find such a family, though? They had no option but to walk, and walk, and walk, until they came across one.

So they did walk, on and on and on, until the firm ground became softer under their feet. Soon they found themselves in the midst of a muck-thick swamp, where will-o'-the-wisps danced and bullfrogs croaked. They became frightened. But on they went.

When the sun came up the next morning, and the swamp still showed no sign of coming to an end, Gretel began to worry. "I think we'll be lost forever!" she said.

Hansel said, "And there's no food anywhere."

But Hansel was wrong. For just then, the two children saw a marvelous sight. There was a house, right in the center of the swamp. Its walls were the color of chocolate cake, and its roof glittered under the rising sun like icing. Slowly, the two hungry travelers approached it.

"I'm hungry," Hansel said.

"Me too," Gretel agreed.

"It looks like cake," Hansel said.

"It smells like cake," Gretel agreed.

"Let's eat it!" Hansel cried.

"*Mmmggrgmmm!*" Gretel tried to agree, but her mouth was already full of fudgy, moist chocolate cake.

Just then, the door to the house flew open, and a woman in a baker's apron appeared on the front step. "Who's eating my house?" she bellowed. Hansel hid a handful of cake behind his back. Gretel had chocolate all over her face.

"No one," Hansel said. Gretel nodded, swallowing.

But the baker woman's face softened when she saw the two children. "You must be lost, to be in the middle of the swamp all by yourselves! Are you hungry?"

Gretel nodded and tried to sneak another handful of cake from the wall of the house.

"Well, don't eat my house!" the baker woman laughed. "Come in and I'll fix you a proper breakfast!"

So the children came in, and she made them goose eggs and wild boar bacon and good thick brown German bread with butter. They were so full after breakfast, and so exhausted from having walked all night, that the kindly baker woman put them in her bed and let them sleep all day.

When they awoke, a wonderful meal of sausages and potatoes and cold milk was laid out before them.

"But I'm not hungry," Hansel said.

"Oh, you must eat up and regain your strength!" the baker woman told him.

So the children ate. The food was delicious.

The baker woman asked the children what their names were.

"This is Gretel," Hansel said as he shoveled a disgustingly

large amount of potatoes into his mouth. "And I'm her brother, Hansel."

Then the baker woman wanted to know how they had come to her house. They were careful not to let her know that they were royalty, lest she return them to the castle and their murderous parents. But they did tell her that their parents had cut off their heads (which the baker woman didn't believe). And that they were looking for a kind family where no one would ever do that to them again.

"And where we can eat cake whenever we want?" Gretel added hopefully.

The baker woman smiled and brought forth an enormous chocolate cake.

"Hooray!" Hansel cried. Gretel shoveled a fistful into her mouth.

The two children stayed with the baker woman for many weeks. Every day, they ate three enormous meals, plus a snack between lunch and dinner, and one before bedtime. They could eat whatever they wanted, and they did. Gretel shoveled chocolate cake into her mouth continuously, smearing it onto her pink cheeks like war paint. Hansel wasn't much better.

One night, as the children lay in bed with horrible stomachaches, Hansel said to his sister, "Do you think this is Heaven? The baker woman does all the work, we can eat as much as we like, and we never have to do anything."

"It must be Heaven," Gretel said.

Then Hansel said, "Gretel, do you miss our parents?"

Gretel tried to think if she did or not. But she couldn't tell. She was too busy eating the wall.

It wasn't Heaven, of course. For, as you well know, the baker woman was planning to eat them.

But she wasn't a witch. The Brothers Grimm call her a witch, but nothing could be further from the truth. In fact she was just a regular woman who had discovered, sometime around the birth of her second child, that while she liked chicken and she liked beef and she liked pork, what she really, *really* liked was *child*.

I bet you can figure out how this happened.

When I was little, my mother used to say, "Oh, you're so cute! Look at those little arms! Look at those little legs! Look at that little tookie!" (That was my mother's word for my bottom.) And then she'd say, "I'm going to eat you up!" And she said it like she meant it.

Has your parent ever said something like that to you? Most

parents say that kind of thing all the time, you know. It's totally normal. Just be careful not to let them actually *taste* you.

Well, the baker woman's children tasted so good to her that she decided to spend the rest of her time trying to find others to devour. She liked them nice and plump, so she always made sure to fatten them up before she ate them. Which is why she was treating Hansel and Gretel as she was.

Why else would she allow them to wallow around all day, giving them nothing to do, nothing to work for, nothing to learn? Why else trap them in a house of chocolate cake and let them eat to their hearts' content, never warning them that they would become fat and lazy, like pigs in a sty?

Parents are supposed to help their children to grow wise and healthy and strong. The baker woman was doing the opposite, plying the children with so much food and giving them so little to do that they could not help but become weak and heavy and dull instead.

Dull enough that Gretel didn't question when the baker woman asked her to clean out the large, mysterious cage in the back of the house, and then slammed the door shut on her. Heavy enough that Hansel didn't feel like going outside to see where his sister had gone. Weak enough that, when the baker woman told Hansel that they would be fattening Gretel up for just one more week, and that then they would eat her, Hansel could do nothing about it.

And then the day came to eat Gretel. "I think we'll roast her," the baker woman said. "A little rosemary, some salt, and we'll put her in the oven for three or four hours. Then her meat will positively fall off the bone."

She brought the fat Hansel down to her basement, where there stood an enormous oven. "I need you to check if this is hot enough, sweetie," the baker woman said. "I'm going to start heating it, and you get inside. When I can smell your skin roasting, I'll know it's ready for your sister." She shoved Hansel inside and closed the oven door.

The oven became hotter and hotter, and Hansel began to sweat. Then a delicious smell wafted to his nostrils.

Oh no! he thought. *I'm cooking!* He sniffed at the air. *And I smell delicious!*

But he wasn't cooking. It just was the remainder of a leg of goose that he'd hidden in his trouser pocket from last night's dinner and had forgotten to eat before he fell asleep. It was so hot in the oven that the skin was crinkling. The baker woman smelled it, too. She came down and opened the oven door. "Are you cooking yet?" she asked. But Hansel shook his head and took another bite of the goose leg. The baker woman frowned and closed the oven door.

I probably should have said yes, he thought. *Oh well.*

He finished off the goose leg and continued to sweat. Soon, another delicious smell rose to his nostrils.

Oh no! he thought. *Now I'm cooking for certain!* He sniffed at the air. *And I smell delicious!*

But he wasn't cooking. It was three strips of bacon that he'd tucked into his socks at breakfast. It was so hot in the oven that the fat was sizzling and popping. The baker woman smelled it, too. She came down and opened the oven door. "Are you cooking yet?" she asked. But Hansel shook his head and ate the second strip of bacon. The baker woman frowned and closed the door.

I probably should have said yes, he thought. *Oh well.*

Hansel finished off the bacon and continued to sweat. Soon, yet another delicious smell rose to his nostrils.

Oh no! he thought. *I* must *be cooking now! And I smell delicious! Just like chocolate cake!*

This time, he was right. He *was* cooking. And he *did* smell just like chocolate cake, because he had eaten so much of it since coming to the baker woman's house. The baker woman smelled him cooking, came downstairs, and opened the oven door. "Are you cooking yet?" she asked.

But Hansel shook his head. "I don't think it's hot enough in here," he shrugged. "That smell was just some chocolate cake I'd stuffed in my undies."

"Not hot enough in there!" the baker woman huffed. "Let me see!" She crawled into the oven, pushing Hansel out of the way. "Feels plenty hot to me!" she said.

Hansel had crawled out of the oven while the baker woman was crawling in. He looked at her—pink and mean and sweating, sitting in the enormous oven.

"Hey!" she shouted at him. "What are you doing?"

Something dim flickered in his food-addled brain. "I'm saving myself and my sister," he said, "from another terrible parent." And then he closed and locked the oven door.

"Hey! Let me out!" the baker woman shouted at him. "Hey, you stupid little kid, let me out!" Hansel stared through the grate on the oven door at her.

The baker woman began to sweat more. Her face was burning. "I'm sorry!" she cried. "I'm sorry for what I've done. I don't want to die! Just let me out! Let me out!"

Hansel's face softened.

"Please? Please! I could die in here! I could die!"

Hansel began to feel sorry for her. But he certainly wasn't going to let her out.

He walked upstairs and out to the back of the house, where he found Gretel sitting in the dirty cage. "Are you hungry?" he asked.

She looked up.

"Dinner's in the oven," he added.

But Gretel wasn't hungry.

And besides, he was only kidding.

The End

Now, that's not a bad little story. But it is a crime, a *crime*, that that is the only part of Hansel and Gretel's story that anybody knows.

Yeah, yeah, nearly getting eaten by a cannibalistic baker woman is bad. But not nearly as bad as what's to come.

Speaking of which, the little kids might have liked that one. Or at least, they probably could have sat through it without screaming their heads off.

In fact, if any little kids heard that story, that's just fine. Hi, little kids. But things get much worse from here on. So why don't you go hire a babysitter, and let's do the rest of this thing alone.

The
Seven
Swallows

*O*nce upon a time, a man lived with his wife and seven sons in a cozy little hut in the middle of a small village. The sons were strong and good, and the wife was kind and loving, and you would think that they would be a very happy family. And, for the most part, you would think right. But the father wasn't quite as happy as he could have been. You see, he wished for a daughter more than anything in the world. But since he and his wife had tried for one seven times, and failed each time, he was now resigned never to get his wish.

Imagine his surprise, then, when one evening a boy and a girl knocked on his door and asked if they could come and live with him. They explained that they had run away from two different homes together; one where their parents had cut off their heads, and the other where a wicked woman had tried to eat them. The man nodded at them like you nod at crazy people.

But, they said, when they saw this cozy little house in the center of the village, with candlelight flickering in every window, they decided that it was a better house for a family than either a palace or a cake-house, and that any parents who lived inside would probably love them and not try to hurt them. So they had decided that they would like to live there for the rest of their days, if that was okay with the man and his wife.

Well, the man was delighted (maybe their heads really had been cut off. So what? Who cared!). He breathlessly ushered in Hansel and Gretel—for that's who they were, of course—and told his wife to prepare them dinner. Then he ran to tell his seven sons to go to the town well for water for the bath.

"Who's taking a bath?" the eldest one asked.

"Your new brother and sister!" the father shouted with joy. "Now hurry!"

The boys were puzzled by this, certainly. But they knew their father had a terrible temper when he was angry and were afraid to displease him, so together they hoisted the great wooden tub onto their shoulders and ran to the well.

The man's wife laid a steaming plate of boiled meat and potatoes before the children.

Gretel hesitated. "Will we have to do chores if we live here with you?" she asked.

The woman was kind but firm when she said, "You will."

"And go to school?"

"Of course!" the woman scolded.

"Good." Gretel thanked the woman for the food, and she and Hansel, slowly and not-at-all greedily, began to eat.

Meanwhile, the father wondered where his new children's bath could be. For the seven brothers, in their haste not to displease their father, had lost their grip on the tub and sent it tumbling into the well. "He'll be furious!" the eldest whispered, while the youngest cried, "He'll beat us for certain!" They crowded around the well, wondering what they should do.

At home, their father was getting more impatient by the minute. "Where are those foolish boys?" he whispered to his wife as she worked in the kitchen. "Our new daughter and son will be wanting their bath at any moment!"

When, a short time later, the boys still were not home, the man swore and said, "They are useless! I wish they would all just turn into birds and fly away!"

At that very moment, in the village, the seven boys turned

into seven swallows and wheeled into the evening air. They flew past their house's kitchen window before disappearing into the nearby wood. The woman saw this and turned on her husband in a fury. But he said it was all for the best, and that they had always wanted a daughter more anyway, and he made her promise never to tell their new children what had happened. For, he said, what good could come of their knowing? Reluctantly, and with tears in her eyes, his wife agreed.

At first, things were fine in the cozy little house. Hansel and Gretel's new parents were very kind and always took especially good care of Gretel. But the children soon began to worry. Their new father was happy, but their mother seemed to bear a great sadness with her wherever she went. Gretel in particular loved her new mother very much. She could not stand to see her so upset.

"Tell me, Mother!" she would say. "Tell me what's wrong!" But always her mother would pretend to laugh, and shoo her away.

There were other strange things that Hansel and Gretel began to notice. Their room had seven beds in it, and more than once they asked their new parents what these seven beds were for. Their parents told them it had been a guest room before Hansel and Gretel had come to live there, but Gretel didn't believe them.

"Who has seven guests all at once, and makes them sleep in the same room?" Gretel wondered aloud.

Hansel was less worried. Once he came upon their new father staring at the seven empty beds in their room with a tear hanging from the end of his nose. But he didn't know what to make of it. Besides, he was happy to be in a place where your father wouldn't cut off your head, and your mother wouldn't try to eat you.

But Gretel grew more and more uncomfortable living there. She heard whisperings about the town. "Oh, nice children, yes. But such a sacrifice! All seven sons at once!" And she wondered more and more about their new mother's sadness.

In time, one of the children of the town told Gretel the whole story, and a few other children, wide-eyed and earnest, confirmed it. Everyone in a little town knows everything about everybody.

"We can't live here anymore!" she implored her brother that night. "It's our fault that the boys were turned into swallows! We must do something!"

Hansel was devastated. "Aren't there any good parents in all the wide world?" he muttered.

"It's my fault," Gretel said, for the children had told her how badly the father wanted a daughter. "He did it because of me." She turned to Hansel. "We've got to find them."

"What? Who?"

"The swallows."

"How are we going to find seven little birds out there?" he said, and gestured at the window of their room. The gesture was so weak and small that it made "out there" seem utterly unconquerable.

Gretel didn't know. But she did know that they had to try. Otherwise her heart would break from guilt. Hansel didn't think they had any hope of finding them—but he had suddenly begun to worry that this new father would wish *him* into a swallow, too. So he agreed to go and try.

When the night was heavy and their new parents were asleep, Hansel and Gretel slipped out into the darkness to find the seven swallows. They walked all night and all the next day and all the next night. "I still don't know how we're going to find them," Hansel sighed.

Gretel shook her head. But as the sun came up the next morning, dazzling their eyes, Gretel said, "I know! The sun! She sees us everywhere we go. She must know what happened to the seven swallow boys! Let's ask her!"

Hansel thought she was crazy. On the other hand, he didn't have any better ideas.

So Hansel and Gretel climbed the tallest tree they could find, until they were right up near the sun. They tried to speak to her, but she was too hot and terrible. They had to hide their faces. Hansel tugged on Gretel's shirt. "I think she eats children," Hansel whispered. Gretel thought he was probably right. They climbed back down the tree and started walking again.

That evening, as the moon rose above the trees, Gretel said, "The moon sees us just as much as the sun. And he's not so hot and terrible. Let's go and ask him!" So they climbed the tallest tree and got as near as they dared to the moon. The moon wasn't hot and terrible. Instead, he was cold and creepy. "Fee-fie-foe-fesh, I think I smell child-flesh!" he said.

Hansel and Gretel hurried down the tree as quickly as they could.

Yes, the moon really did say that. No, I didn't think the moon ate people, either. But it says so, right in the original Grimm. And I looked it up. It's true.

Scared and dejected, Hansel and Gretel walked on until they came to a beautiful lake that shimmered in the starlight. "We've been walking forever," Hansel said. "We'll never find them! Can't we just give up?"

But Gretel's guilt was bubbling like a boiling pot inside her. "It's my fault that our new mother's sons have disappeared!" Gretel moaned.

She began to weep, and her tears fell into the shimmering lake. When they landed, they shook the reflection of the stars on the water, waking them from their glittering sleep.

"Whose tears have woken us?" the stars asked. At first Hansel and Gretel were scared. Did stars eat children, too? But the shining stars seemed far nicer than the blistering sun or the creepy moon. So Gretel told the stars all her troubles.

"We've seen the seven swallows flying," the stars said. "They live in the Crystal Mountain. You can save them, but it will take great courage and sacrifice. The mountain is months of hard travel from here. If you decide to go, take this chicken bone with you. It will open the door to the Crystal Mountain and let the seven swallows out." Just then, the children noticed a chicken bone beneath the surface of the water, at the edge of the pool.

Hansel did not want to go. "Months?" he bleated.

But Gretel said, "Please, Hansel!" And she grabbed his arm and held it tight. At first Hansel resisted, but once he saw that his sister would not change her mind (and that he was losing feeling in his arm), he reluctantly agreed to go.

So Gretel put the chicken bone in her pocket, and the two children journeyed for a month and a day, and then another, and then another. They passed through dark forests and sunny fields, blazing deserts and muck-filled swamps. They grew much during their travels and became strong and lean from hardship and perseverance. Gretel carried her smoldering guilt with her always, but it was bearable so long as she knew she was doing something about it.

Finally they came to a massive mountain range and proceeded through the whipping snow and wind. The peaks of the mountains rose up white and sharp all around them, like the craggy teeth of some stone beast. Above, the sky was pale and clear but so, so cold. Their cheeks became red and chapped, their lips blue with frostbite. Hansel wanted to turn back. But Gretel would not let him.

After days and days of climbing, they finally arrived at the Crystal Mountain. It was tremendous—the most wonderful thing they had ever seen. Its crystalline crags rose straight up from the ice and snow that lay at its base. Kestrels and merlins twirled around its peaks, screaming to the skies.

"It's beautiful," Hansel murmured, and Gretel nodded wordlessly. "At last," he said. "I couldn't have gone any farther."

Before them was an enormous door made of ice, with a keyhole just about the width of a finger—or a chicken bone. Gretel reached into her pocket.

She found nothing. She reached down farther, and farther, and farther, until she felt the cold alpine air swirling around one of her fingers. She had a hole in her pocket.

She had lost the bone.

They looked all around for it. "When did you last have it?" Hansel asked. "Last night? The night before?" But Gretel couldn't remember, and she became more and more afraid. Soon she collapsed on the ground and sobbed until her little body nearly broke. "All these months," she wept, "for nothing! What I've taken you through! And I've failed our new mother!" Hansel wrapped Gretel up in their traveling cloaks, and, as the night came on, lay down beside her to sleep.

But Gretel could not sleep. After many an hour her tears subsided. But still she could only think of her failure. Her guilt burned her like the scouring wind. And then the stars came out and reminded her of her failure again, and she felt so guilty, so foolish, so worthless that she could not even look at them.

Near daybreak, she looked down the long path that she

and Hansel had trod. They would have to go back now, having accomplished nothing. Months and months more of suffering. And all the while, her guilt would throb inside of her.

Suddenly, Gretel ran to the door of the Crystal Mountain and began to bang with all her might, pleading to be let in. She banged so hard, in fact, that she cut herself on a shard of ice. She woke her sleeping brother, who offered to tend to her wound. But she refused. "I'd rather make it worse," she said.

She picked up a sliver of ice, as sharp as a knife, and brought it down on her middle finger, severing it from her hand. Hansel stared, aghast. Gretel's face was white and her voice trembled when she said, "Now I can make things right." She was bleeding swiftly from where the finger used to be, but she stood and walked, resolute and grim, to the door of the mountain. She picked up the finger, slid it into the keyhole, and turned it.

The door opened.

I'm sorry. I wish I could have skipped this part. I really do. Gretel cutting off her own finger? And putting it into a keyhole?

If there was any question about the truth of this part of the story, I would have left it out altogether. Maybe she could have found another chicken bone. Or maybe, if she wished hard enough, and said some magic word, the door could have opened on its own.

But there's no doubt about the finger. Besides, if I left it out you'd be wondering why Gretel had only nine fingers at the end of this book. Which reminds me of another question you're probably asking.

Why did the door open?

I don't know. A finger is enough like a chicken bone, I guess? Why a chicken bone, even, in the first place? Again, I don't know. I have no idea why either a chicken bone or a finger should open the Crystal Mountain. (As for the location of the Crystal Mountain, that's quite clear, and if you have any interest, I'd be happy to share it with you. Just write me.)

Now I've got to say something about cutting off one's own finger, in case any young children are still reading or hearing this tale—which would be almost beyond belief, given all of the terrible things that have happened so far. Cutting off your finger, my young friends, is about the stupidest thing you could do. Don't do it. *You* won't be able to open *anything* with your finger. Only Gretel could.

Why?

I've already told you. I don't know.

Though it may have something to do with sacrifice.

As the door swung open, a storm of brown wings knocked the children back onto the snow, and seven swallows swirled out of the mountain. They settled on the ground, their black eyes studying Hansel and Gretel curiously.

"It didn't work," Gretel said incredulously, her bleeding hand really beginning to hurt.

Hansel watched the swallows walk mutely around on the white snow. He didn't know what to say. They were still birds. He wanted to cry.

After a few moments of painful, confused silence, Gretel bent down beside the smallest swallow. "It's time to go home, little bird," she said. "Your mother misses you." The swallow held her in its black gaze.

Hansel thought back to the boys' father, and suddenly he remembered that tear hanging from the end of his nose. "Your father misses you, too," he told them.

Suddenly the claws on the swallows' feet softened, and their thin black legs began to lengthen and grow thick. Wings stretched outward, until fingers appeared at their ends, and then there were wrists, elbows, shoulders, and all the rest. The swallows' black eyes paled, their feathers turned to hair and clothes, and finally, in a circle around Hansel and Gretel, stood the seven brothers.

"He misses us?" the littlest one asked. Hansel and Gretel, amazed by the transformation, nodded dumbly.

The boys began to rejoice, and, after a fit of hugging and laughing and cheering, the eldest turned to Hansel and Gretel and invited them into the Crystal Mountain, where they all drank warm milk and ate Black Forest cookies and talked late into the evening.

The next day, the brothers invited Hansel and Gretel to return home with them.

Hansel and Gretel said they wanted to talk it over. As soon as they were alone, Hansel said, "I don't want to, Gretel. I don't want to go with them." Gretel nodded solemnly. Hansel sat down heavily on the ground. "I don't want to live with a father that could do something like that to his children." He thought back to all the other parents he had known. His own father had cut off his head. The baker woman had tried to eat Gretel. And then this new father had wished his sons into birds.

Gretel was thinking the same thing. She felt the space on her hand where her finger had been. She looked up at Hansel. He was leaner and stronger than she had ever seen him. They had both grown much over the difficult journey to the Crystal Mountain.

"Perhaps we don't need parents at all," she said. "Perhaps we can take care of ourselves."

"Yes!" Hansel cried, leaping to his feet. "Let's live without any terrible parents at all!"

And so the two brave children, now a little older, and a lot wiser, and with only nineteen fingers between them, set off into the world to find a life that they could call their own.

I won't even bother saying "The End" anymore. You know it isn't.

As for this next story, it is really dark. Frightening things happen. You may feel upset—I'm talking to the big kids now.

And as for the little ones, if they are still around, I warn you, I *plead* with you: Make them go away. Don't let them hear this story. They may have nightmares. No, they *will* have nightmares.

At least read it yourself first. Then, if you think they can take it, maybe, *maybe* you can read it to them. And then you have only yourself to blame if they can't sleep for a week.

Brother
and Sister

*O*nce upon a time, a brother and a sister clasped hands (one of which was missing a finger) and strode out of the white mountains, across green hills, and into a large and wonderful wood.

Trees towered above them like the pillars of Heaven—strong and straight all the way up. Birds sang and flitted by their faces. Little rodents—chipmunks, squirrels, mice—dashed in and out of the underbrush. A fawn appeared and looked at them from behind a stand of ferns, and then bounded off after his mother. Everything was greener here, more full of life, than anywhere Hansel and Gretel had ever been.

The vibrant power of the place began to take hold of the children. Hansel rushed out ahead of his sister, bounding through the ferns, and then running back again, like a dog that's been let off his tether. Gretel laughed and sang and collected bluebottles and daisies and other wildflowers.

"We could make a life here!" she shouted to her brother.

Hansel hooted with delight and took off after a low-flying blackbird.

Soon the two came to a clearing where there stood a magnificent tree. It rose to such heights that they could barely make out where the lowest branches began, though they could see, if they looked really hard, a crown of green far above them. Gretel jumped when she noticed, in the wood of the tree, what appeared to be a woman's face. It was made of bark, with brown hair wrapping around its smooth cheeks and wide eyes. Gretel walked up to it, mesmerized.

"What a magnificent tree," she said.

"Thank you," the tree replied.

Now you might have expected Gretel to jump, or Hansel to fall backward over a conveniently placed log, but neither did. The tree's voice was so gentle that neither child was startled at all.

"Welcome to my wood," she went on. "It is called the Lebenwald, the Wood of Life."

———

That's pronounced LAY-ben-vault. Go ahead and say it. German is fun.

"Plant something," the tree went on, "and watch it sprout before your eyes. Spy on the wild beasts, and see them leap and bound and grow. You, too, will grow here, and live, and be happy." Her woody eyes drifted over them, and then she asked, invitingly, "Do you plan to stay?"

Hansel looked to Gretel. She nodded and said, "If you don't mind."

"I don't mind." The tree smiled, and then added, "But I ask of you one thing. Please, take no more than you need. Life here exists in a delicate balance. Do not upset it." Then she told them that, less than a league hence, lay a lovely spot where they could build their home. The children thanked the tree, because it is always best to thank talking trees. Then they bid her farewell and started for the place she had told them of.

They soon came to a small clearing. Some large stones were partially buried in the earth there, and nearby a brook burbled and babbled over smooth rocks. The sun shone in through the green leaves. Hansel and Gretel agreed that this was the place the tree must have meant. They gathered fallen branches and fronds of fern and laid them against the great rocks so that a little hut was formed, half green, half gray. They gathered more ferns, as well as moss and leaves, and made two little beds for themselves, side by side. Then Gretel gathered seeds to begin a garden, and Hansel gathered nuts and berries for supper. That night, they feasted.

Gretel swore that nothing could make her happier, and Hansel agreed. They decided that they needed nothing else—certainly not parents—and that they would be able to live happily, just like this, for the rest of their lives.

Yeah, right.

(Oh, did I say that out loud?)

The next day, Hansel was out gathering food for dinner as Gretel tended their garden. He walked beneath the towering trees, and heard the birds singing as they flitted by, and he thought, *What life! What excitement! I want to be part of it all!* Just then, a brown rabbit ran across his path. Hansel felt his legs twitch. Before he knew it, he was pursuing the rabbit through the underbrush.

As the sun set that evening, he walked back into the clearing,

ADAM GIDWITZ

exhausted but as happy as the chirruping birds. He had the rabbit in his hand. It was dead. He placed it before Gretel on the ground. "Now we must make a fire," he said, "and eat."

But Gretel was upset. "Why did you do it?" she asked. "We don't need this!" Suddenly Hansel felt sorry for having killed the small beast, though he had enjoyed hunting it so. They made a fire and cooked the rabbit and ate it so it would not go to waste. But Gretel made him promise not to kill any more animals. "We have everything that we need right here," she said. "Remember what the tree told us." He felt bad, and promised.

But the next day, as he walked through the woods looking for nuts and berries, he saw a tiny baby fawn, nosing a stand of fern. His legs began to twitch again, and his heart began to race. He remembered what his sister had made him promise. He told himself to turn away. But there was something about the air here, the color of the green, the musty scent of the wood, that made him want to burst as he watched the tiny fawn among the fronds of fern. He couldn't help it. In a flash, he lit off after the frightened creature.

As the sun set that evening, he walked back into the clearing, exhausted but as happy as the little animals that run among the underbrush. Over his shoulder was slung the fawn. He placed it before his sister on the ground.

"What have you done?!" she cried.

He attempted to calm her. "Now we can eat meat for a whole month!" he said. "And I won't have to kill another animal for a long, long time!"

She looked at him in disbelief, and then began to weep bitterly over the dead fawn. "Why did you do it?" she muttered. "We have all we need here. Remember what the tree said." Hansel suddenly remembered once more, and remorse swept over him.

That night, he tossed and turned. He was furious at himself. Hadn't she told him? Hadn't they both told him? Don't take more than you need. He and Gretel had eaten as much of the fawn as they could that night, and it looked as if they hadn't even touched it. Now the carcass lay outside on the grass attracting flies, its stench wafting over their beautiful clearing. As Hansel stared at it, he vowed to be his own master, and not let his impulses carry him away again.

The next day, before he went out to find fruit, Gretel made him swear on his very life that he would kill nothing else. He swore it, and hugged her and kissed her for being so good and so forgiving, and he promised he would do nothing violent ever again as long as they remained in this forest. She kissed him on his forehead, as if he were much younger than she, and sent him off for the nuts and fruit.

ADAM GIDWITZ

He spent the whole day basking in the lovely green light of the leaves, picking berries and storing them in his tattered shirt, which he had tied around his waist like an apron. He felt the peacefulness and calm of the forest, and he wondered why he hadn't always been able to feel it, why he had been overcome the last two days with that uncontrollable animal lust.

And then he saw a white dove perching on a nearby branch. Something tingled in his legs and arms. "Don't," he told himself. "It's wrong." He started to shake. "Go home. Turn away and go home." But he found himself creeping in the direction of the dove. The berries fell to the ground.

As the sun set that evening, he walked back into the clearing, exhausted but as happy as a sated wolf. Blood covered his arms and his face, and he carried in his hands the broken, eviscerated carcass of the white dove. Gretel screamed when she saw him. "What have you done!" she cried. "Hansel, what's wrong with you?" Hansel stopped. Then he looked down at the dead bird. He noticed that his arms were covered in blood, and his shirt was stained with a mix of blood and berry juice. He wondered where the berries were. Gretel began to cry. Hansel, confused and upset, placed the dead dove at her feet. She backed away from it, covering her face. He looked at her, and felt awful. But not as awful as he had felt the night before. He turned and walked back into the woods.

Gretel saw Hansel only infrequently after that. Occasionally, as she was out collecting berries, she saw him running through the forest after some animal or other. At first he had stopped to speak with her—just a few words each time. But soon she noticed that words were not coming as easily to him as they once had, and he was ever and always looking off over his shoulder, or following the flight of birds with jerky movements of his head. Soon he wasn't stopping to speak with her at all.

She found animal carcasses littered all over the forest. Some were half-eaten, others barely touched. Once, she found a wild boar, larger than Hansel, with its neck broken. She wondered how Hansel had the strength to do such a thing. She wondered how he had the heart to do it.

She saw him only in flashes now. A blur of skin through the trees. The scream of a dying animal, and then a howl of delight. She thought he looked different. He was growing hair on his face, on his back.

She was frightened to be in the wood by herself, particularly at night. She heard howling—howling that she hadn't heard when they'd first come to the Lebenwald. She wondered if it was Hansel.

She stayed closer and closer to the hut for fear of seeing him. Then, one day, he wandered into the clearing. Gretel stared. He walked bent now. He had hair all over his body—his arms, his back, his face, his chest. Wordlessly, she offered him a handful of berries and nuts. He snarled at her. She dropped them and hurried into the hut. He growled and stalked around the clearing for a few minutes. Gretel wondered if he would kill her. But he left.

There were fewer animals in the forest these days. Gretel heard no birds in song. She saw no small rodents darting in and out of the underbrush. No deer nosed the stands of fern.

And then, early one morning, a hunting party—a duke and his household—entered the wood. They blew their horns and their hounds bayed and barked. Gretel feared for herself. But more than that, she feared for Hansel. She crept into the hut and stayed there all day, hoping he would come to her.

The dogs and huntsmen scoured the forest for some sign of animal life. To their surprise, they found none. All day they searched, and all day they found nothing. The duke became angry and impatient. And then, at dusk, he saw a strange, hairy, hunched creature peering out from behind a large tree. "There!" he bellowed, and instantly the dogs were in pursuit.

Hansel fled through the wood, thrilling at the terror of the chase. The dogs bayed at his heels; the horns sounded all around him. He dodged this way and that, panting, growling, laughing, howling. *What fun!* he thought. *What tremendous, terrifying fun!*

At last, he came to the edge of a brook. Across the way, the duke sat astride his horse, his bowstring pulled tight, an arrow nocked and aimed at Hansel. The animal-boy stared curiously at the sweating, red-faced man holding the strange bent stick. Then there was a snap and a hiss like a snake. An arrow flew through the air—a straight, simple harbinger of death. Hansel watched it all the way to his chest, to exactly where his heart was. It buried itself there. He felt a searing bolt of pain and fell to the forest floor.

The huntsmen tied the strange, dead animal to a pole and carried him triumphantly back to the duke's manor.

The next morning, Gretel ran through the wood looking for her brother. For a long time she found nothing but broken branches and paw prints. Then, at last, she came to the brook and saw the earth stained a copper red, and the rocks at the water's edge spattered with blood.

She ran to the tree with the face in it. "My brother has been killed!" she cried. "He has been killed!" But the tree would not speak to her. Gretel fell to the ground and sobbed and sobbed. She was alone, in a great forest, in a dark tale. Her father had tried to kill her. She'd been nearly eaten by the baker woman, and had cut off her own finger. And now her brother, Hansel, was dead.

She would not stay in that forest, not now. "I need to go back to people," she said, wiping tears from her face. "To grown-ups."

As she left the Wood of Life, she saw a bird alighting in a tree nearby. Soon she could hear the sound of birdsong again. But it only made it hurt more. They only came back, she knew, because Hansel was dead.

We're at one of those places in the story—and they happen in nearly all stories, of any kind—when things seem to be really, really bad. When it feels like, if things get much worse, you won't be able to listen anymore.

When I was little, I used to call this part "the sad part." I knew it would happen in every story, and I knew it always ended eventually, and I would repeat, "This is the sad part this is the sad part" over and over until it was done.

And so, as I was piecing these stories together, I came to this part. And I realized that this was "the sad part." I repeated this to myself again and again, to try to make it not feel so terrible.

But it didn't help. It never does. It still hurts when a character you love dies, and another is left all alone in the world.

Nevertheless, I will tell you, as I always tell myself, that things will get better. Much, much better. I promise.

Just not quite yet.

A Smile
as Red as Blood

*O*nce upon a time, a little girl named Gretel walked down a wide, lonely road all by herself. She was as sad as a little girl can be, for the person whom she loved most in all the world was gone.

After a time, she came to a small village that stood in the shadow of another great wood. This wood was as big as the last one, but no two woods could have been more different. Where the Wood of Life had been bright, inviting, and alive, this one was dark, forbidding, and dead. So forbidding that almost no one went in. And exactly no one came out.

It was called the Schwarzwald—the Wood of Darkness.

———

That's SHVAHTS-vault. In case you were wondering.

But the little village that stood near the Schwarzwald was not dark at all. No, no: It was ringed by trees that, when Gretel arrived, had just slipped into their golden robes of autumn. Laughter was in the air, as was the smell of wood burning in fireplaces and apple cider frothing with cinnamon.

Gretel walked down the town's single road, looking in the warm windows of the little houses, wishing that someone might invite her inside for some food, cider, and a little human comfort.

But all the doors remained closed to Gretel. She was very tired, and very, very lonely, and on the verge of giving up. She sat down and all her troubles overwhelmed her. She began to cry.

Presently, the door to one of the houses opened, and a silver-haired woman came out. She went up to the little girl crying by the side of the road and asked her her name, and why she was all alone. Gretel told her that she and her brother had long ago run away from home, but that recently her brother had been killed and she didn't know where to go or what to do. The woman reached out to hold her, and Gretel fell into her arms and buried her face in the woman's neck. She took Gretel into her home and washed her and picked the knots from her hair and gave her some old, but clean, clothes.

Some weeks went by. Gretel had no thought now of where else she should go, or what else she should do. For what sense did it make to do anything now that Hansel was gone?

And that is how Gretel came to live with the silver-haired widow in the little village.

Soon Gretel was just another child there, and, though she carried a great sorrow around with her, she put on a brave face. It was the time of the harvest, and everyone worked all day long, including Gretel. In the evenings, when the autumn air became cool, the villagers would gather in and in front of the town tavern and drink and laugh and converse, while the children ran about in their games. But Gretel had no heart to play. So instead she sat by the grown-ups and listened to their talk.

There was one grown-up in particular whom Gretel liked listening to. He was a young man, cheerful and kind. And he was very handsome. He had long black hair and green eyes flecked with gold that seemed to dance in the light. And it seemed to Gretel that the young man liked her, too, for whenever he saw her looking at him, he would smile with lips of deep red, before she, blushing, could turn away.

So she sat near him always and marveled at his easy jokes and his careless laughter and his wonderful eyes. Occasionally he would leave the grown-ups in the tavern and go out among the children. He would tease them gently, and lift them up, and all of them, particularly the girls, loved him.

Sometimes a child would bring to the handsome young man a toy that was broken. It would be a porcelain doll with a finger that had cracked off or a wooden king that had lost its head. The handsome young man would draw from his pocket a tattered piece of twine. He would hold the toy between his knees and tie the twine around the broken place. When he unwound the twine, the toy was as good as new. The children would cry aloud and clap their hands, and the handsome young man would smile. Then he would go back to the tavern with the grown-ups.

Each day, as the sky turned from pale blue to rich purple to black, Gretel would watch the handsome young man say his farewells, slip out the tavern door, and disappear into the darkness. Out of the village. All alone. She wondered where he went.

Well, one warm afternoon, when the last of the barley had been brought in from the fields, Gretel sat by the door of the tavern and watched the men play their favorite game. They played like this: One man balanced a mug on his chin, and everyone else tried to throw coins into it. If the mug didn't fall, the man got to keep all the coins. If it did, he had to buy everyone a drink.

It was the young man's turn to have the mug on his chin, and Gretel watched as he weaved about like a snake being charmed, trying to prevent the mug from falling. Just then, one of the young man's friends appeared at Gretel's shoulder.

"Give him a shout," the friend whispered. "See if he can hold it then."

Gretel thought this was a funny idea. So she called the young man's name loudly.

He was startled, for never before had Gretel spoken to him. He turned to her, and as he did, the mug went crashing to the ground. The men cheered, and the man who had put her up to it threw his head back and laughed till he was red from his collar to the top of his bald pate.

But the young man's golden green eyes were wide, and suddenly he rushed at Gretel. His hands were stretched out before him like claws. Gretel screamed as he caught her hard around the waist.

And then, in a moment, she was swooping through the air, her long blond hair streaming out behind her, and his strong arms holding tightly onto her hips. And he was laughing—a beautiful, joyous laugh, his head thrown back and his eyes shining.

He placed her on the ground again and smiled at her, and Gretel was breathless. He rubbed her head as if she were a puppy, and then he turned to lead the other men into the tavern.

Gretel had been fascinated by the young man before. But in that moment, when he held her high in the air and his golden green eyes were sparkling and his red lips were curving and he was laughing—laughing with her, and her alone—well, at that moment, Gretel had passed beyond fascination. In that moment, Gretel had fallen in love.

It wasn't real love, you might say. Just a child's infatuation.

You might say that. But if you did, it would prove that you are already old, and that you don't remember what it is like to be a child at all.

Every day after that, Gretel made sure to be near the handsome young man with the green eyes and black hair and red lips. He would talk to her and make her laugh and steal apples from the harvest barrels for her. And she wondered why she should be so lucky as to get all of this attention from him.

One day, soon before the great Harvest Feast, as the day's work in the orchards was coming to a close and all the ladders were being folded up and taken in, Gretel noticed a large, beautiful apple still hanging from the bough of a tree up above her head. She tried to jump for it, to grab it and put it in the barrels before a bird saw it and pecked holes in it. But it was too high for her to reach. So she called to the handsome young man, asking him to come over and pluck it. He came and smiled at her, but it was too high for him, too. So he took her by the hips and lifted her into the air, and she gasped—as she always gasped when he touched her—and then she was high enough in the air to reach the apple. And she picked it.

And then, instead of putting her down, he threw her into the air. Gretel screamed—but not in fear. And he caught her and threw her up again, and she was laughing. And he threw her up a third time, but this time he threw her too near an overhanging branch, and she reached up to protect her head, but too late, and she cried out in pain. When he lowered her to the ground, red blood was running in a narrow rivulet down her face. Her forehead had struck the branch and left a deep cut just above her eyebrow. She was having trouble seeing out of her left eye through the steady stream of blood. The young man knelt before her. He gazed at the cut. Very gently, very slowly, he applied his lips to it, and he sucked the blood away. Gretel did not know what to think of that. Then he took from his pocket the piece of tattered twine that he used to fix the children's toys, and he wrapped it around her head, so that it ran crosswise over the cut. He smiled at Gretel. And when he took the twine away and wiped the blood from Gretel's face, she saw that the bleeding had stopped and that her head no longer hurt at all.

Now, dear reader, I seem to detect in you a growing unease about this handsome young man. I must say, I think that is very unfair of you.

Do you suspect a flower, just because it is beautiful?

Or a doctor, for his mysterious healing power?

Or the postman, because you don't know where he sleeps at night?

Very unfair indeed.

Oh, and while I'm thinking about it, you should go ahead and rehire that babysitter that came by for the previous story. Make her take the little ones out to a movie this time. A G-rated movie. Or an R-rated movie, for that matter. Whatever it is, it probably won't be as bad as what you're about to read.

I know, you don't believe me. "How much worse could things get?" you ask.

Believe me. Much worse.

As Gretel and the handsome young man walked in from the orchard that night, they talked about this and that—the weather, the apple crop, the upcoming Harvest Feast—until suddenly he turned to her and asked her if she didn't wonder where he lived. Gretel, shyly, replied that she did wonder sometimes. He asked if maybe she would like to see his house. Her heart fluttered, and she told him she would like to very much, and she thanked him for the kind invitation. And then she asked the handsome young man where his house was.

"A little ways into the forest," he said.

"In the forest?"

He laughed. "You're not afraid of that silly old forest, are you?"

"No," she lied.

"I'll leave a path of ashes for you to follow. How's that?"

Gretel's heart floated up near her mouth. "That's good," she said.

But that night, when she returned home and told the widow that she was going into the Schwarzwald to visit the handsome young man, a great fight began. The widow forbade her from going. It was not right for a child to visit a man's house in the first place, she said. And the fact that it was in the Schwarzwald? Did Gretel know nothing of that place? Was she a fool?

Gretel was furious. She raged and cried all that night. The next day, her face red and puffy, she told the handsome young man that she could not come, that the widow would not allow it. He smiled and told her not to worry, that they were still friends. But he talked to her less that day. She watched him from afar. Rarely did his gaze turn to meet hers.

He's forgetting me, she thought.

At the end of the day, the handsome young man turned toward the tavern without even glancing at Gretel—as if she no longer even existed.

Just before he disappeared inside the tavern door, Gretel ran and caught him by the arm. "I'll come," she whispered fiercely, urgently. "I'll come tomorrow."

The young man hesitated, and then smiled and went into the tavern.

ADAM GIDWITZ

———

Gretel returned home more determined than ever. She told the widow that she was going on the morrow, and that there was nothing she could do about it. They fought more that night, but Gretel was implacable. Early the next morning, she rose and prepared to go.

But she found the widow, arms folded sternly across her chest, standing before the door. Gretel ran and pushed past her, squeezing under her armpit and then breaking into a run once she made it past the door frame.

"Gretel!" the widow cried. "Gretel!" But Gretel ignored her, and ran out of the yard and into the dirt road.

Then, from the doorway, the widow cried, "Take these!" Gretel slowed and looked back. The widow held a bag of lentils in her hand. Cautiously, fearing a trick, Gretel walked back into the yard.

"Scatter them on the ashen path," the widow said mournfully. "In case it rains."

Gretel walked to the edge of the Schwarzwald and peered in. She felt a shiver skitter down her spine. At the wood's edge the trees had the bright red and yellow leaves of high autumn. But

Gretel could see that a little farther in the branches were mostly bare. The path of ashes snaked deep into the wood and out of sight.

For a moment, Gretel hesitated. The wood was an evil place. Everyone knew that. What if she just turned around, she wondered, and did not go? What then? He would think she was a coward. Or worse—he would think that she did not care. No, Gretel could not allow that. She breathed deep. Then she plunged into the darkness, scattering lentils as she went.

As she walked, the air became colder, and within minutes the sunlight was almost entirely blocked by the trees. Gretel began to feel frightened. Branches hung like the claws of dead men. Clouds of gray mist passed by, looking for all the world like lost souls. The trees around her were gnarled and scarred, mutilated by time. No bird sang.

The branches' long fingers became longer as Gretel walked, and soon it seemed that they were trying to grab her hair and her cheeks, scratching and tearing into her soft skin. She tripped on the twisted roots that reached up from the ground like corpses in a graveyard come back to life. Then it began to rain, as cold and sharp as needles falling from the sky. The rain struck the wood of the trees, making eerie sounds almost like words. Gretel stopped and listened. The words seemed to say:

> *Go home, little girl, go home;*
>
> *To a murderer's house you've come.*

For a moment she stopped and considered following the rain's advice. But then she shook her head. "You're being foolish," Gretel told herself. "Rain can't talk."

No, of course it can't. The moon can eat children, and fingers can open doors, and people's heads can be put back on.

But rain? Talk? Don't be ridiculous.

Good thinking, Gretel dear. Good thinking.

She went on through the darkness, ducking to avoid the clawing branches, and still she scattered the lentils behind her. Finally she came to a clearing.

In the center of it stood a tall, dilapidated house. It had once been painted black, but now the paint was peeling, revealing the rotting wood beneath—which was black, too. The stone roof was high and steeply sloping, with a long row of unlit windows poking out from beneath the slate.

Before the windows, from the eaves, hung cages. In almost

every one there perched a white bird, like a dove—but filthy, covered with brown stains and molting feathers. As Gretel stepped into the clearing, one called out in a voice that sounded more like a crow's than a dove's:

> *Go home, little girl, go home;*
> *To a murderer's house you've come.*

Then another repeated it, and another, their raspy voices ringing out together in horrible chorus:

> *Go home, little girl, go home;*
> *To a murderer's house you've come.*

Pssst!

Gretel!

GRETEL!

What are you doing? Turn around! Go home! Go home!

You would go home, wouldn't you, dear reader? *You* wouldn't be taken in by such a man as this. You would turn right around and leave.

Tell me you would. Say you would.

Oh no, you wouldn't.

Not with such an object of your fascination and adoration there waiting for you—for you alone.

Haven't you ever had that enchanting friend—the coolest boy, the older girl—and he or she seemed to like *you*? Of all people, *you*?

Imagine that he or she is in that house. Waiting for you. For no one but you.

What would you do?

What *wouldn't* you do?

Gretel followed the path of ashes up to the stairs. The heavy ebony door stood slightly ajar. "Hello?" she called. No answer. Slowly, fearfully, she pushed the door back and entered the front hall. All was dark, save a faint glow from a stairway that descended to the cellar. She followed the dim light belowground, carefully placing one small foot after the other on the creaking stairs.

She found herself in a filthy old kitchen. Dirty pots and pans lay in piles on the stone floor. Chairs were overturned. In the middle of the room was a plain oaken table, with a large copper-colored stain. Gretel thought it looked like blood. Off in one corner, a great cauldron boiled, and crouched over it was an old woman with an iron shackle on her leg.

"Hello?" Gretel said uncertainly.

The woman turned. Her face was like worn leather; her teeth were rotting in her gums. She glanced fearfully at the steps that led above. "Who are you?" the old woman hissed. "What are you doing here?"

"I'm here to see my friend," Gretel answered, her voice atremble.

The woman stared at her. "Through the wood?" she asked. "By yourself?"

Gretel nodded.

"Oh, poor girl," the old woman muttered as she came nearer. "You are brave to come all this way. But you must flee."

Gretel's eyes grew wide, but she did not move. "I want to see him," Gretel said.

The old woman sighed and touched the girl's cheek, which was bleeding from the clawing branches. "Oh, my dear, does your friend have long black hair, green eyes that dance with flecks of gold, and lips as red as blood?"

Gretel nodded.

"Then, my dear, you have befriended your death."

The old woman paused, and then went on. "He is my son,

though what kind of son would keep his mother locked up as a prisoner, I do not know. He is evil—an evil magician, a warlock. He invites girls to this house, and he . . ."

No little children around, right? Like I asked? Are you sure? Check under the bed. At this point, they're usually hiding under the bed.

No? Okay, so long as you're certain. . . .

"He invites girls to this house, and he reaches down their throats and rips their souls from their bodies, and he traps the souls in cages in the form of doves, to let them rot under his eaves. Then he hacks the girls' bodies to pieces to make our supper."

The old woman smiled sadly and reached out to touch a lock of Gretel's golden hair. "Such a brave and pretty girl. But such a fool."

Suddenly, a crash rang out above. The woman's eyes went wide, and, without another word, she pushed Gretel behind an enormous stack of dirty pots and scampered back to her cauldron. At that very moment, the handsome young man with the green eyes and smile as red as blood appeared at the foot of the steps.

He had a girl by the hair.

Dear Readers:

I'm sorry for what follows.

He threw the girl on the oaken table, and from a nearby cupboard produced a filthy iron cage. Then he reached his hand into the girl's mouth until his arm was buried deep in her throat. Slowly, painfully, and with great struggle from the girl, he pulled forth a beautiful white dove. The dove fought the young man as he shoved it in the filthy cage and slammed the door shut.

The girl's body was still.

Now you might want to close your eyes.

He lifted an ax that hung on the wall, and Gretel, peering through a gap between a filthy pot and a filthier pan, watched her handsome, wonderful, funny friend hack the girl's body into bits and toss each piece into the boiling cauldron. His blunt butcher's knife rose and fell, rose and fell. He licked the blood from his hands and sent piece after piece sailing into the pot.

Each piece, that is, save one.

On the girl's left hand there was a lovely golden ring, inlaid with rubies, red as rubies can be. He tried to remove the ring so that it would not ruin the stew, but it wouldn't come off. Finally, in a rage, he hacked the finger clean off her hand and hurled it across the room. Gretel watched, dumbstruck, as it tumbled through the air, over the enormous pile of pots and pans that she was hiding behind, and landed squarely in her lap, ring and all.

Somehow, she did not scream.

The young man picked up the cage and started for the stairs. "I'll be back in a moment, Mother," he said. "See that my stew is ready!"

As soon as he'd gone, the old woman ducked behind the pile of pots and pans. "Go, my dear!" she hissed at Gretel. "Run away and never come back!" The little girl needed no further encouragement. She fled up the stairs and out the door. But she came to a stop on the steps of the house. The rain was falling fat and wet and hard now, and the ashen path was utterly washed away. Even the lentils would be buried in the muck that was made by the heavy rain. Gretel had no way to get home.

But then she noticed something incredible. The lentils had sprouted. In the little time she'd been in the house, green shoots had come up from the wet soil, and now a pale green path marked her way back through the wood. She followed it as fast as her feet would carry her.

When Gretel arrived at the widow's house, she went straight to her room and locked herself in.

The widow came to the door, leaned her head against the door frame, and asked Gretel if she was all right. Gretel didn't answer.

She had her face buried deep in her pillow. As if it were still before her eyes, she could see the young man's bright blade, slicing through the air toward the innocent girl on the table. And yet it wasn't the young man's blade at all. It was the blade of her father's sword, and the innocent girl was Gretel, her white neck exposed to the cold, flashing steel. She saw the young man's face and her father's face, as if they were one.

"Are there no good grown-ups anywhere?" she cried.

She wished she had her brother beside her. But he was gone. Dead.

And it's my fault, she thought, and suddenly she realized that she had thought this all along. *It's my fault. We shouldn't have run away from home. We shouldn't have eaten the walls of that house. And I shouldn't have let Hansel go into the woods alone—not once, not twice, and certainly not three times!* Her whole body throbbed. *All the grown-ups want to kill me! I don't blame them! What is wrong with me?* Her little body shook. *Why am I so bad?*

"Oh, don't be stupid," said a voice.

Gretel looked up with a start.

She was alone in the room. So who had said that? She looked under the door. The widow had gone away. She turned and faced the window.

There, sitting on the window frame, was a black raven. She gazed at it curiously.

He tapped his black beak against the glass. And then he said, "Do you mind if we come in?"

Gretel wiped her face and advanced to the window. "We?"

"Yes, my brothers and I."

Gretel opened the window and in fluttered three ravens, as black as could be.

"You shouldn't tell her she's stupid," said the second raven to the first. "It isn't polite."

"Even if it is true," said the third.

The first raven cleared his throat. "We happened to be flying by, dear girl, when we noticed that you were upset. We felt bad."

"Personally responsible," added the second.

"Accidentally complicit," said the third.

Gretel, who had had a very long day already, plopped down on her bed and stared.

"You see," the first raven continued, "all the misfortune that you and your poor brother have experienced is really the result of a . . . well, I guess you'd say, an *indiscreet* conversation that the three of us had." He cocked his head apologetically.

Gretel continued to stare.

"Indiscreet," the second whispered.

"What about it?" the first replied.

The third rolled his eyes. "*Indiscreet*, dear girl, means we shouldn't have been talking about what we were talking about where we were talking about it."

"Oh, that was helpful," said the second. And then, "Why don't we just explain it to her?"

And so, once the three ravens had settled their feathers and found comfortable perches on the windowsill, they told Gretel the whole story, from the very beginning. They told her about her grandfather's dying wish, and how her father had found the portrait anyway, and then how he had stolen her mother . . .

"He did *what*?" Gretel interrupted.

"Moving right along," said the second raven.

Then they told her about their indiscreet conversation, and how her father's servant, Faithful Johannes, had heard it and used it to save her parents' lives.

"You see," the first raven continued, "any wedding between your parents was destined to be cursed."

"The three of us know *all about* destiny," interrupted the second raven.

"It's sort of what we *do*," said the third.

"They were destined to be cursed," the first began, "though what they did to you children . . ."

"That goes a little beyond the scope of the curse, I'd say," finished the second.

The third raven added quickly, "But it certainly isn't *your* fault."

"It's probably ours," said the first magnanimously. "Had we kept our black beaks shut, none of this would have happened."

Gretel scrunched up her face. "Because my parents would have died before Hansel and I were born?"

"Exactly!"

"That doesn't seem much better," Gretel pointed out.

"Hmm," said the first. "I guess that's right."

"No," Gretel said. "It's my fault. If Hansel and I hadn't run away from home, he wouldn't be dead. And we never would have killed the baker woman, and the father never would have wished his sons into swallows, and—"

The third raven interrupted her. "Do you remember why you ran away, Gretel?"

She looked into his black eyes and nodded.

He said, "Seems like a pretty good reason to me."

Gretel stared past the three ravens and out the window, at the red and orange leaves that balanced on the ends of branches like tears. After a while, the third raven said, "Well, we really should be going. More flying around to be done, letting people's fates out of the bag."

"Anything else we can answer for you before we go?" said the second raven.

"It really isn't my fault," Gretel said.

"We are unable to lie," the first raven replied. "So it must not be." And with that, the three ravens beat their black wings against the air and flew out the open window.

Gretel fell back on her bed.

It wasn't her fault.

She had the sudden impulse to take all of the sadness that had been crushing her and hurl it away—to hurl it at those who had caused it in the first place—to make them feel the pain, and know it, and understand it. And understand her.

Slowly, she reached into her pocket and let her hand close around something that was small and cool and turning blue.

The next day, the village was all merriment. Tables were set all about with bread and beer and cider, as well as harvest gourds and autumn leaves and other signs of the festive season. Neighbors spoke cheerily about the cool, clear weather, and little clouds of steam puffed from their mouths. Smoke rose from chimneys, and the smell of roasting sausage, topped with apples, wafted over the gathering.

The handsome young man stood with the other men, drinking beer from a great mug and laughing about this and that. Children ran to and fro. Soon the sausages were ready, and heaping platters were brought to the tables. Gretel quietly emerged from the old woman's house, her hands buried deep in the pocket of her dress.

Everyone went to their seats at the tables, and the master of the town stood and delivered a few fine words. A couple of the older men did as well. Then the handsome young man stood up, raised his glass to the women, and said they were as beautiful as any women in all the world. All the men cheered heartily, and the women blushed and smiled.

And then, to everyone's surprise, Gretel stood up. "Can I say something?" she asked timidly. Even standing, she was smaller than most of the sitting adults.

"Get up on the chair, honey," one of the villagers told her. So she stood on her chair.

"I want to tell you—" she began. But then she stopped. She looked at the handsome young man. He was smiling at her. But then she glanced down at his hands—hands that could tear a girl's soul from its body—"a dream," Gretel said. "Just a dream that I had."

The villagers murmured with approval. Once upon a time, you see, dreams were thought to possess hidden truth.

"I dreamed that I went into the Schwarzwald," she said. "But as I walked through it, and the rain hit my face, and the roots tripped my feet, I heard the trees whisper, *Go home, little girl, go home; to a murderer's house you've come.*"

The villagers started with dismay, and the young man was staring at Gretel with a very strange expression on his face. Gretel glanced at his powerful, magical hands, and said hastily, "It was only a dream.

"I came to a house in a clearing. And white birds hung in cages from the eaves. And they chanted, all together: *Go home, little girl, go home; to a murderer's house you've come.* But I went inside the house and followed a light into the cellar, where I found

ADAM GIDWITZ

an old woman wearing a chain of iron. She told me to flee, and that the man who lived there was her son, and a warlock—and a murderer."

The young man suddenly leaped to his feet. All the villagers stared at him. Sheepishly, he sat back down.

"It was just a dream," Gretel said cautiously. "Just a dream.

"Then the man came home. And," she added quietly, "he looked just like you." And Gretel pointed to the handsome young man—who was staring intently at her and had begun chewing on his fingernails like a madman.

"He had a girl and he was dragging her by the hair. He threw her onto a table and pulled a pure white dove from her mouth and put it in a cage. It was only a dream. And then he took an ax and he chopped the girl to bits. It was only a dream. And he licked the blood off his fingers and threw the bits of the girl into a boiling cauldron. It was only a dream!" The villagers were now talking to one another excitedly, pointing first at her and then at the young man.

"Except one piece didn't go in the cauldron," she went on. "The girl's finger had a golden ring, with rubies red as rubies can be. He threw the finger in a rage, and it tumbled through the air and fell right in my lap." She paused. The villagers were now silent, waiting for the conclusion of Gretel's tale. The handsome young man's shoulders were rising and falling, rising and falling, and his eyes were wild. Gretel, standing on the chair, put her hand into her pocket and drew it out again. "And here it is!" she said. She held the blueing finger, with the ring still on it, in her hand.

The young man leaped from his chair and began to chant the words of a dark curse, but before he could finish someone came up behind him and knocked him unconscious with a tray of sausages. Then the oil was prepared, and a villager was sent to find the poisonous snakes.

Because the best way to kill a warlock is to cook him with poisonous snakes in a cauldron of boiling oil.

Obviously.

But before the handsome young man could be thrown into the cauldron, Gretel went up to his unconscious body and slipped her slender hand into one of his pockets. She withdrew the tattered, bloodstained piece of twine. She put it in her own pocket, and then nodded to the men of the village, who hoisted up his limp body and threw it into the hissing vat of oil and snakes.

As the evil young man's life came to an end, somewhere deep

in the forest a magic shackle was broken, and an old woman was set free. And around the eaves of a dark house, a hundred doves burst forth from their cages and fell to the ground, young women again.

Gretel returned to the feasting table with all the other villagers. They comforted her and marveled at her courage. At the end of the meal she approached the widow and, after apologizing for being so willful and disobedient, told her that she would soon be leaving.

"Where do you plan to go?" the widow asked.

Gretel thought about it. At last, she said, "On."

There, that one didn't end so badly. Yes, it was pretty gory in the middle, but Gretel didn't lose any body parts, and nobody died—at least, nobody we really liked.

In fact, things start getting better right here. So if you're still feeling sad—about Hansel or anything else—don't stop now. In fact, if you're still feeling sad, now's the time to keep going.

(On the other hand, if you're feeling sick to your stomach because of all the blood, now's a great time to stop.)

The Three Golden Hairs

*O*nce upon a time, a duke returned home from a hunt in a magnificent wood.

In his great hall the lords and ladies of his manor awaited him. Every year the duke brought back a great bounty from his hunt, and the lords and ladies would ooh and ahh, and then be treated to a feast.

There was much excitement when the duke finally entered the hall. The lords and ladies cheered, and he bowed and waved and shook hands all around. Trumpets were sounded, and the huntsmen began to file in.

But the first huntsman carried nothing. The lords and ladies wondered at this—but the duke smiled serenely. The second huntsman carried nothing. Still the duke smiled. The third, nothing. The fourth, nothing. The lords and ladies began to wonder if this was some kind of joke. One lord even ventured to laugh, but the duke turned an eye of such withering scorn on him that the laughter immediately ceased, and the laughing lord later sold all of his belongings and moved to a neighboring kingdom.

Finally, there were two score huntsmen in the great hall, and not one of them carried a dead animal of any kind.

The duke turned to his audience. "Ladies and gentlemen!" he said—and he meant this quite literally—"I present to you the worst hunt—and the best—that I have ever had. The fewest creatures! But the rarest prize!"

In came two more huntsmen. Between them they carried a pole. Hanging from that pole was the strangest, most grotesque beast that anyone had ever laid eyes on—it looked like something halfway between a wolf and a man, a bear and a boy.

Ladies screamed. Lords cried aloud. A servant fainted dead away.

The huntsmen cut the dead creature down from its pole. Two more huntsmen approached it with gleaming knives as the duke looked on proudly. They would take off the beast's hide and head and mount both on the duke's wall.

———

Warning: this next bit is kind of gross.

The huntsmen dug their knives into the beast's skin just below the jaw and began to run their blades between the fur and flesh. Their hunting knives shone red as clumps of meat and animal hair stuck to their blades. The lords and ladies watched with disgusted amusement. The duke giggled with glee. Who else would have the hide and head of such a monster?

Soon the huntsmen skinning the beast began to gape. One sprang back from the creature, muttering, "It isn't right! It isn't holy!" Another huntsman stepped in for him, but soon he fell away, too, crying that there was something "terrible unnatural" about the beast. Finally, the task was left to one huntsman alone—a grizzled old man who bared his teeth and steadily, carefully finished the skinning.

He stepped back from the carcass so that all could see it before he cut off its head. Gasps echoed through the hall.

For beneath that beastly skin was another layer of skin—human skin. And beneath that beastly form was another form—a human form. The blood-soaked form of a boy.

Carefully, the grizzled huntsman returned to take off the beastly head. He sliced into the skin—but instead of severing the neck, he gently peeled away the top layer of hide and fur. After a few minutes' work, he stepped back again.

In the middle of the floor of the castle's great hall there lay a naked, bloodstained boy.

"I will cut no more," the huntsman said. "He's breathing."

After the commotion and hubbub had died down, and a doctor had come and gone, and the duke had bragged to one and all that not only was he the only hunter to ever kill a beast-boy, but that he was also the only hunter ever to not kill one (which left more than a few people scratching their heads), the question arose of who would take the bloody, unconscious boy home. A lord and lady who had never had any children of their own soon volunteered, and the boy was moved to their manor and cared for as well as a boy can be.

When, after a few days, the boy finally woke up, he informed them that his name was Hansel.

Hansel was comfortable in the rich, sprawling manor, with a lord and a lady for parents. But he was not happy.

Not a moment passed when he did not wonder what had

become of Gretel. He felt ashamed at how he had acted in the Wood of Life. She had been so good to him, and he had been selfish and irresponsible. It made him sick to think of it.

He could not sleep for his shame. Each restless, sweaty night, he lay awake, staring into the darkness. Then, in the morning, he would rise and wander through the manor like a ghost.

Where was Gretel? What had happened to her? He feared it was something terrible. And if so, it was all his fault. He wanted to scream. How, how could she ever forgive him? It was like a private Hell of his own thoughts, and he knew no way of escaping it.

And then, one night, as he lay in bed and tossed and turned and sweat, he thought, *I will never do anything like that ever again. I will find Gretel and make things right with her. I will be responsible. I will be good. I swear it.*

And because he wanted it so, so badly, he was.

And he felt better.

Wait, don't tell me, dear readers. This sounds implausible to you.

Of course it does. Having never experienced such a thing yourself, it naturally sounds ludicrous. He wished to be good, and so he was? Just like that?

Yes. Just like that. There is a certain kind of pain that can change you. Even the strongest sword, when placed in a raging fire, will soften and bend and change its form. So it was with Hansel. The fire of guilt and shame was just that hot.

Trust me on this one. I know this from personal experience. I hope that you never will, but, since you're a person, and therefore prone to making horrible, soul-splitting mistakes, you probably will one day know what this kind of guilt and shame feels like. And when that time comes, I hope you have the strength, as Hansel had, to take advantage of the fire and re-shape your own sword.

Once Hansel had sworn to be good, his life was quite bearable. The lord and the lady were fine parents: They cared for Hansel and spoke kindly to him and fed him good food. They had a wonderful library, and Hansel enjoyed sitting in it, reading books about knights and damsels, dragons and giants. He knew he couldn't stay in the manor forever, for he needed to find Gretel. But until he regained his strength he was very happy to stay with these new grown-ups. There seemed to be nothing wrong with them.

—

Ah, it makes me sad to even say it. Is there ever nothing wrong with grown-ups? Certainly not in these stories.

Maybe in real life there are perfect parents and amazing adults who will never, ever disappoint you. But Once Upon a Time, no grown-up was perfect. You, my dear reader, have certainly learned that by now.

The Lord and Lady were not perfect, either, of course. Sometimes the Lady had a short temper. Usually the Lord had bad breath.

But worse than these things was that the Lord had a secret—a secret he kept from even his wife. It wasn't a terrible secret— nothing cruel or evil. It was a secret weakness, one that, try as he might, he could not control. The Lord loved to gamble.

He lived every day without giving in to his weakness, but at night, a cold sweat gripped him, and he could not help taking his and his wife's gold from their chest and creeping down to the back room of an alehouse in town and wagering on cards. Sometimes he won. Usually he lost. But never yet had he lost so much that his wife noticed the difference in the morning.

But one night, a stranger joined the game. His skin looked almost red in the dim light of the tavern's back room, and his beard was cut into a point below his chin. He bet with the Lord, and he won. He won and won and won again. The Lord knew he should go home, for his money was gone. But he knew that if he went home having lost all their gold, his wife would discover his secret failing. He was ashamed. He asked the bearded stranger if he could win his money back. The stranger said that he could, if he would wager whatever stood before the fire in his library that night. The man could think of nothing that stood before the fire in his library except his fine mahogany stool. It was a small price to pay for the chance to win all his money back. So he agreed.

The Lord lost. He returned home in despair. He walked into the library where the fire burned, wondering if there was some way to hide the loss of all that gold (and the stool) from his wife. But as his eyes fell on the stool before the fire, he saw Hansel sitting on it reading a book.

The Lord thought back to the gambling stranger, to his reddish skin, his pointed beard, and his strange wager . . .

Knowledge smacked the Lord over the head like a tray of sausages. He staggered and fell to the ground. Hansel rushed to his side.

"Gambling . . ." the Lord said.

"Are you all right?" Hansel asked.

The Lord's face was pale, and his eyes stared up at the ceiling blankly. "I was gambling with the Devil."

———

The next morning, they waited for the Devil to come and collect his due. The Lord wrung his hands and apologized to Hansel over and over, as the Lady buried her face in her kerchief and wept. But Hansel just stood there, nervous and numb. It was too strange, too incredible to believe. He had been gambled away to the Devil? What did that mean? What would he have to do?

He wouldn't have to *do* anything, of course. If you are gambled away to the Devil (and this is a matter of public record—I'm certainly not making it up), you are damned to excruciating pain for all eternity, and no matter what you do, no matter how good you are, or how many times you ask, "Please pretty please with a cherry on top?," the Devil will never, ever, ever let you out. It's excruciating pain from the moment you arrive in Hell until the moment after eternity.

But Hansel did not know that. Which, for the moment, was probably best.

After a time, the Devil arrived at the manor. He wore a walking coat and carried a cane and had tiny spectacles that sat on the end of his nose. And his hair looked like a hundred thousand strands of shining gold. He approached Hansel and frowned.

"He's a bit pure, isn't he?" the Devil said, and sniffed. "He smells . . . *good.*"

Hansel swallowed hard.

"Oh, yes, he's very good," the Lord said. "Too good to go to Hell."

"Would *you* rather go?" the Devil said swiftly, turning on the Lord.

"Oh, no, no," the Lord said. "No, take him!"

The Devil smiled and muttered to himself, "You'll be there shortly anyway."

"What?" the Lord said.

"Nothing . . ."

The Devil turned to Hansel. "Well, you're so good and so pure it makes me sick. I can't touch you, and I wouldn't want to anyway. It'd take me *weeks* to get the stench of you off me. So report to the gates of Hell in three days' time."

Hansel gathered his courage and said, "What will happen to me in Hell?"

"I love it when they ask that," the Devil said, smiling. "You'll be in excruciating pain for all eternity, and no matter what you do, no matter how good you are, or how many times you ask,

'Please pretty please with a cherry on top?,' I will never, ever, ever let you out. It's excruciating pain from the moment you arrive until the moment after eternity."

Well, the cat's out of the bag now.

He came very close to Hansel, and Hansel could feel the heat of the Devil's skin. "And if you're not at the gates of Hell in three days' time, I'll flood the whole valley with fire, and everyone in it will die. And then I'll find your soul, of course, and take my due."

Now Hansel wanted to cry. But he held his breath, stuck out his chin, and said in his bravest voice, "I'll be there."

And the Devil said, "I know." Then he turned for the door, waved a single pinkie at the Lord, and was gone.

In a forest near the Lord's manor there wandered a very old man. He had a long nose, a bent back, and lips that puckered around a toothless mouth. He was searching for two children, a boy and a girl, who had been lost long ago.

He was about to sit and rest his aching bones beneath the

branches of a comfortable-looking tree when, from a distance, he heard the sound of someone crying. He followed the sound to the foot of a great elm, where he found a boy cradling his head in his hands. The old man felt pity for the poor boy, so he comforted him, and asked him if he needed help.

"No one can help me," the boy moaned. "I must travel to the gates of Hell in three days' time and deliver myself to the Devil— to be in excruciating pain until the moment after eternity."

"Hansel?" the old man said.

The boy looked up. "How do you know my name?"

For a moment, the old man said nothing—he just stared at the boy's head of curly black hair and round eyes, dark as charcoal. Then he said, "Never mind, I thought you were someone else."

He sat down beside Hansel gingerly and frowned. "So," he said, "you must go to Hell?" Hansel sniffled hard, wiped the tears from his face with the back of his sleeve, and began to tell the old man why.

When he finished, the man was staring at him intently. "It's not a lost cause, my boy. Nearly. But not completely." He stopped.

"Yes?" Hansel asked.

"Well," the old man said, "it is said that in Hell the Devil can have no power over one who has three of his golden hairs."

Hansel thought back to the bespectacled Devil with the thin strands of gold on his head.

"But how would I get them?" Hansel asked.

"That, I have no idea. But I can take you to the gates of Hell—I know where those are. And I can guide you back if you ever come out."

"That's very kind of you," Hansel said, staring into the man's unlovely face. And then he said, "But now can you tell me how you knew my name?"

The old man didn't answer. Instead, he slowly got to his feet and began to walk. After he had gone a little way, he turned and saw that Hansel was still sitting on the ground under the great elm. "Well," the old man said, "do you want to go to Hell or not?"

They journeyed all day, until, when the sun was low in the sky, they came to a small city, ringed by walls of stone. The old man asked the guard if he and Hansel could stay within the city walls for the night.

"No one stays in this city," said the guard. "For our fountain of wine no longer flows, and we are all in mourning." And he told them of a magical fountain that had once given wine without cease, until one day it didn't. "Devil knows why!" the soldier said, throwing up his hands.

The old man was about to turn away from the city gate when Hansel said, "I'm going to see the Devil in Hell. Perhaps I can ask him why, and if ever I escape, I will come back and tell you."

The soldier scratched his head. "I didn't mean the Devil *literally* knows why. . . . It's an expression."

"It is?" Hansel replied. "Oh. What does it mean?"

"It means—" the soldier began, but stopped. "Wait, are you really going to Hell?"

Hansel nodded and so did the old man.

The guard stared at the little boy. "Never mind. Just come in."

The next day, the old man and Hansel walked until the sun was low in the sky, and again they found themselves at the gate of a city with walls of stone. Again the old man asked the guard if he and Hansel could stay.

But the guard said, "No one stays in this city. For our tree of golden apples is now barren, and we are all in mourning." And he told them of a magical tree that had once given golden apples without cease, until one day it didn't. "Devil knows why!" the soldier said, throwing up his hands.

So Hansel said, "I am going to see the Devil in Hell. Perhaps I can ask him why, and if ever I escape, I will come back and tell you."

The soldier scratched his head. "I didn't mean the Devil *literally* knows why. . . . It's an expression."

"People keep saying that," Hansel replied. "What does it mean?"

"It means—" the soldier began, but stopped. "Wait, are you really going to Hell?"

Hansel nodded, and so did the old man.

The guard stared at the little boy. "Never mind. Just come in."

On the third day, the man and Hansel walked until, when the sun was low in the sky, they came to a river that could only be crossed by ferry. But the ferryman refused to take them over. "I've been in this ferry for seven years, and I can't get out!" the ferryman said. "I'm sick to death of it! My arms are exhausted, I haven't slept well in ages, and you don't even want to *hear* about going to the bathroom."

"Why can't you get out?" the old man asked.

"Devil knows why!" the ferryman said, throwing up his hands.

So Hansel said, "I am going to see the Devil in Hell. Perhaps I can ask him why, and if ever I escape, I will come back and tell you."

"I didn't mean the Devil *literally*—wait, did you say you're going to *Hell*?" the ferryman asked. "But why?"

"The Devil knows," Hansel replied.

The ferryman scratched his head at that. But then he said, "Well, if you promise to come back and tell me why I'm stuck here, I'd be happy to take you over." And so he did.

At last, as the sun was disappearing beyond the edge of the horizon on the third day, the old man and Hansel arrived at the tall, black doors of Hell. Hansel's knees began to knock gently against each other. The doors to Hell led directly underground, and there was no handle or knocker. They were just smooth and black. Like eternity.

"Be brave," the old man said. "And get those three golden hairs."

Hansel said, "I will." But he wasn't sure he believed it.

Hansel's hand was trembling so badly it took him three tries just to knock on the great doors. But as soon as his knuckles hit them, they swung open, and two pairs of long red arms grabbed him and thrust him inside. The doors slammed shut behind him.

Faithful Johannes sat down on the ground to wait. He wondered how long eternity was.

Hansel stood just inside Hell's doors, staring all around him. He was in what looked like a cave. It had a low, heavy ceiling hung with long spires of rock; down these spires dripped a red liquid that looked, for all the world, like blood. But though there was a ceiling, there were no walls. Hansel could see forever in every direction. A thousand paths stretched out from where he stood, paths that wound past millions upon millions of craters of bubbling, boiling, liquid fire. In each crater a sinner screamed as red-armed demons drove him under the liquid fire's surface. The sinners kicked and struggled as they were held below. Sometimes the demons would allow them to rise, and the sinners would scream and cry and say that they were sorry and please let them out, please pretty please with a cherry on top, and then the demons would push them down again to suffocate and be burned.

"Look fun?" said one of Hansel's two demon guides. Then he led Hansel between the pits of fire, over a path that glowed like embers. The soles of Hansel's feet began to scorch, and he hopped from foot to foot and winced. But far worse than the pain in his feet was the chorus of screaming sinners bursting forth from the pits and then being shoved back down again, like hellish jack-in-the-boxes.

As they passed one crater, a heavyset woman burst from beneath the bubbling fire and screamed, "Oh pretty please, stop!" Hansel stared at her. It was the baker woman. She saw him, too. "Hansel!" she cried. "I'm sorry! I'm so sorry! Tell them to stop!

Please tell them to stop! Please! Pretty please!" A demon with a pitchfork shoved her back under the surface of the boiling fire.

Hansel slowed beside the pit. He hated the baker woman. She was bad. He was glad she was being punished for what she'd done—to them and to all the children she must have eaten before they met her. *Yes*, he thought as he watched her bob to the surface again, scream, and then plunge back into the torture below. *Yes, punish her.*

But when she came up again he saw the fear in her face, and the remorse, and the pleading. She deserved to be punished. But not like this. And not for eternity.

"Would you please stop?" Hansel said.

The demon with the pitchfork turned to Hansel. "What?" he hissed.

Hansel swallowed hard. He held his head high. He stared straight into the demon's eyes. "Please," he said. "I've forgiven her. Stop punishing her now."

For a moment, the demon looked paralyzed. Then he glanced at Hansel's demon guides. The corners of his mouth broke into a smile. And he said, "Nice try, kid. But it doesn't work like that."

The two demons laughed and pushed Hansel on. His eyes scanned the pits, looking for the empty one that he knew, somewhere, awaited him. Up ahead, he noticed someone in one of the pits who, for some reason, caught his attention. It was a young man with black hair and striking green eyes. He wailed and howled each time his face rose above the boiling pit. Hansel looked away.

Finally, they arrived at an empty one. Hansel stood at the edge, looking down into the boiling fire, rimmed with black jagged rock.

Have you ever stood at the edge of water and known that it was going to be really, *really* cold? And you knew you had to go in, but you really, really, *really* didn't want to?

Well, this was kind of like that.

But with liquid fire instead.

Hansel clenched his lips and clasped his sweaty hands together. He closed his eyes. Behind him, he heard the demons chuckling. And then, before they could push him or kick him or strike him with the pitchfork, Hansel jumped in.

Pain. Greater pain than he could ever have imagined. Burning so terrible and unnatural that every inch of Hansel's body screamed to get out of the fire. He began to kick frantically, struggling to get to the surface. Finally he rose above the flames, and there was a split second of relief, as if perhaps the pain was coming to an end. But instantly he felt the sting of pitchforks on his neck and his face, thrusting him back under. He went down again and burned and burned, and the burn was worse this time for having felt, just for an instant, the sweet, cooling relief of the surface. Once more Hansel struggled up and clear of the flames.

He was just about to loose the most lung-cracking scream he had ever produced when he heard one of the demons say, "Give him a minute this time. I like to hear them scream."

Just as the sound pushed past Hansel's throat and over his tongue, he clamped his lips shut. He looked into the demon's narrow, stupid, vicious eyes. And he thought, *For you, I won't*.

After a moment of the sweetest relief imaginable, they pushed him under again, and he was certain his skin was burning off. He kicked up to the surface. The demons looked at him expectantly. But instead of screaming, Hansel concentrated on the howls of the other sufferers.

"I'm sorry!"

"I hate myself for what I did!"

"If only I had been good!"

"Why isn't this one screaming?" the demon said as they shoved him back under the liquid fire.

While he was under again, he realized that, while this was terrible, it wasn't as terrible as all those sleepless nights when he had felt so guilty about abandoning Gretel. At least this was just pain, and not shame and guilt. This was not his fault. He rose to the surface again, and he smiled at the demons.

"This one's defective!" the demon shrieked. And they pushed him back under.

Down and back up, and Hansel smiled. Down and back up, and Hansel smiled. Down and back up, and the demons were pulling him out of the pit.

"What's wrong with this one?" one of them said, and poked him with his pitchfork. Hansel winced but did not make a sound.

"Better take him to the Devil himself," the other demon said. "See what's to be done."

So they took him down another burning path. Hansel's brief sense of triumph was swallowed like a coin slipping into the great dark maw of a well. The Devil himself.

Soon they came to a place where the pits of fire ended, and there began what looked like a quiet, residential neighborhood. They turned on to a wide street, with grass and trees and bushes— but red grass and black trees and red bushes—until they came to a little house with a black picket fence and red walls and black shutters. The demons pushed Hansel to the door. "Go see him," they said. "See if you don't scream then."

They turned away. "I hope we get a screamer next time," one said.

"Yeah," said the other. "That was freaky."

Hansel stood before the door. It was black, like the Gates of Hell, but it was quaint, too, with a knocker that looked like the bronzed head of a kitten. Hansel looked at the knocker more closely. The whiskers were real. It *was* the bronzed head of a kitten.

Avoiding the knocker, Hansel rapped very quietly on the door. No one answered. Cautiously, he leaned his head against it and listened.

Screams—terrible screams, much worse even than those of the sinners in the pits of fire—echoed from inside. Hansel's blood shivered in his veins. "Do it," he told himself. "Do it now." He put his hand on the doorknob and turned it.

Hansel found himself in a living room—sort of like a normal living room. It had a couch before a fire, a wingback armchair, side tables, candles to read by, and a thick rug. But it stank—of sweat and body odor and sulfur all mixed together—it stank so much that Hansel nearly gagged, and was forced to hold his nose and cover his mouth. He looked more closely at the wingback

ADAM GIDWITZ

chair. It wasn't leather. It was human skin. Hansel could see teeth sticking out from one of the seams. He clamped his hand over his mouth more tightly to prevent himself from throwing up.

The screams were coming from the adjoining room. Carefully, Hansel crept up to the edge of the couch. It was made of hair. Human hair. He tried not to think about it. Hidden behind the couch, he could see into the next room. It was the kitchen. In it he saw an old Devil-woman, with a pot and a pan in each hand, cooking and singing. Not screaming. That noise was singing.

Just then, Hansel heard the creaking sound of footsteps on the stairs that led up to the front door. He looked around frantically for a place to hide. His eyes fell on a closet. He ran to it and slipped inside, closing the door quietly behind him. Just then, he heard the Devil's voice.

"Grandmother, I'm home!"

The screaming-singing in the kitchen stopped. "Dinner's ready, my dear." And now Hansel could hear the sound of a table being set.

The Devil helped set the table (for even the Devil helps his grandmother set the table). He stopped and sniffed the air. "Do I smell human flesh?" he asked.

Hansel caught his breath.

"Of course, silly," his grandmother said. "There's a little boy named Hansel, waiting for you in the closet in the living room."

No, she didn't say that. I was just teasing you.

"Of course, silly," his grandmother actually said. "What do you think we're having for dinner?" And they sat down and ate.

Hansel sat in the dark of the closet—surrounded by extra blankets and pillows (he refused to look at what they were made of)—and waited. The Devil ate the supper that his grandmother had made for him—the fingers of sinners, spiced with their guilty tears—and then he yawned loudly.

"Tired from all your wicked trickery?" his grandmother said indulgently. "Come and lie down. You can put your head in my lap, and I'll stroke your beautiful golden hair."

The Devil removed his long traveling coat, took off his spectacles and laid them on a side table, and curled up on the rug in the center of the living room, laying his head in his grandmother's lap. She gently stroked his hair. "Sleep now," she said. "Sleep." Soon he was snoring. After a little while, the grandmother was, too.

Hansel sat there in the dark closet, listening to them snore. Suddenly, he realized this was his chance. Hadn't the old man said that it only required three golden hairs from the Devil's head to escape this place? Carefully, he opened the door of the closet and tiptoed over to where the Devil was sleeping. Ever so gingerly, Hansel reached out and took . . .

A golden hair from the Devil's head.

That's what he's going to take, right?

Right?

Wrong! Are you crazy? The Devil would wake up immediately! And then it would be all over for Hansel, forever and ever and ever.

I hope that's not what you thought Hansel was going to do. If you did, *good luck* if you ever end up in Hell.

Hansel reached out and took the Devil's spectacles from the side table, retreated with them to the closet, and closed the door again. Then he waited there all night.

The next morning, the Devil arose and readied himself for another day of soul-collecting. His grandmother made him a breakfast of human fingernails—scrambled, of course—and packed up his lunch in a bag.

But before he left, the Devil announced that he could not find his glasses. He was furious, for he could barely see without them. "I hardly recognize you, Grandmother!" he shouted. "Where in Hell did I put them?"

"Devil knows!" his grandmother said.

"No, he doesn't!" he shouted. Eventually he stormed out of the house without his glasses, grumbling about telling one sinner from another and wasting a perfectly good day of damnation.

After he was gone, the grandmother went upstairs. Hansel ever so carefully opened the door to the closet. He peered up the stairs. The grandmother was carrying things to the attic. Hansel watched her carry an armload of objects up the stairs—including a crown with a head still attached to it, and something that looked like a squid—and come back down empty-handed. She did it again—this time carrying two giant feet. When she came back down, she was sweating from the heat and strain. She itched her gray hair and then took it off. Hansel grimaced at the scabby, bald head underneath. She disappeared into a room and reemerged without her hair at all, carrying instead a taxidermied child with a lollipop in his nose. As she turned for the attic, Hansel took a deep breath, and he followed her up.

Each of his steps on the stairs made a loud creak, causing him to wince and suck in his breath. But the Devil's grandmother was "singing" again, and she couldn't hear a thing. When she disappeared through the door of the attic, Hansel hurried up after her. She was half buried in boxes and strange objects when he quietly shut the door behind her. To his amazement, relief, and glee, there was a key in the attic door. He turned it in the lock and went back downstairs.

Hansel soon heard frantic banging on the attic door. Then the grandmother began shouting for help. But no one was around to hear. After a lot of banging and shouting, the grandmother seemed to resign herself to a day in the attic, and she quieted down.

Now Hansel made his way into her bedroom. On the dresser before an obsidian mirror stood a wig stand, with the grandmother's gray wig on it. Around it was her makeup—thick black lipstick that looked like a petrified oil slick and blush that looked like dried, powdered blood and fake eyelashes that looked like—no, were—the legs of flies. In the closet were her dresses.

Hansel closed the door to her room.

He came out an hour later, dressed from head to foot like the Devil's grandmother. He wore a billowing black dress, makeup all over his face (he had put it on as best he could, which wasn't very well), and her gray wig. He'd skipped the eyelashes.

In the kitchen, Hansel took what looked to be a pot of human fingers out of the icebox. He put the pot on the stove and turned on the heat. "Leftovers," he said to himself. Then he set the table with forks and knives made of human bone and teeth, and he waited for the Devil to get home.

When he heard the Devil's footsteps trudging up to the door, Hansel began to scream at the top of his lungs. The door opened and the Devil came in.

"Damn it, Grandmother! Can you stop your infernal singing for one bloody instant?"

"Someone's in a bad mood today," Hansel said in his best grandmother voice.

"Without my blasted glasses, there isn't any point looking for sinners. I made a complete fool of myself," the Devil said sullenly.

"Oh, I'm sure you didn't, dear," Hansel said. And he began to ladle the fingers onto the Devil's plate.

"Your voice sounds strange today, Grandmother," the Devil said. "Are you well?"

A cold sweat broke out all over Hansel's skin. "Of course, dear," he said. "Just a little sniffle." And he sniffled twice.

The Devil sat down at the table but immediately turned

on Hansel. "I tell you, it stinks of human flesh in here! It's disgusting!"

But Hansel remembered what the grandmother had said the day before. "Of course it does! What do you think we're having for dinner?"

The Devil took one bite of his dinner and spit it out. "This is revolting. What is it?"

"Leftovers," Hansel said nervously.

"Ugh! I *hate* leftovers!" The Devil stood up and stomped into the living room and plopped down on the couch. "What a horrible day!" he shouted.

Hansel took a deep breath, and then slowly walked into the living room. "Here, dear," he said. "Let me stroke your hair. Everything will be better in the morning." And Hansel sat down in the middle of the living-room rug, just as the Devil's grandmother had done.

The Devil grumbled and laid his head in Hansel's lap. "Grandmother, why are you shaking?" he said.

"The better to rock you to sleep, my dear," Hansel said, and he tried to prevent his teeth from chattering, too.

"Grandmother, will you sing to me?" the Devil asked, his eyelids fluttering closed.

"Certainly, my dear," Hansel said. He swallowed hard. And then he began to scream at the very top of his lungs.

"Grandmother, what a beautiful voice you have," the Devil said.

"The better to sing you to sleep, my dear," Hansel replied.

"Can you stroke my hair?" the Devil said.

With trembling hands, Hansel began to stroke his hair.

"Grandmother, what delicate fingers you have," the Devil said.

"*Shhhh*," Hansel whispered. "Sleep, my dear."

And the Devil slept.

As soon as the Devil's breathing was nice and even, Hansel took one of the Devil's golden hairs between two of his fingers and, trying not to wake him, plucked it out.

"Tar and pitch!" screamed the Devil, sitting up. "Why did you do that?"

Hansel's heart had jumped into his mouth. But he said, as calmly as he could, "I'm sorry! I fell asleep and had a bad dream. I must have grabbed hold of your hair."

The Devil settled himself back in Hansel's lap. "I love bad dreams," he said. "What was it?"

Hansel swallowed. "I dreamed that there was a city with a fountain of wine, but that it flowed no longer, and all of the people were sad."

"Aha! Those old fools!" said the Devil. "I placed a frog right under the fountain. That's what's stopping up all the wine! All they've got to do is kill it. But they don't know that, of course." He chuckled at the unhappiness he had caused and fell back to sleep.

As soon as the Devil's breathing was nice and even again, Hansel took another golden hair between his fingers and plucked it out.

"Sulfur and brimstone!" screamed the Devil, sitting up. "Why did you do that?"

"I'm sorry!" Hansel said. "I fell asleep and had a bad dream again. I must have grabbed hold of your hair."

The Devil settled himself back in Hansel's lap. "Well," he said, "what was it this time?"

"This time I dreamed there was a city with a tree that gave golden apples. But the tree was dying, and it would give apples no more, and all of the people were sad."

"Aha! Those old fools!" said the Devil. "I placed a mouse under the ground at the root of the tree. It's nibbling at the roots and killing it. If they just took the mouse out and did away with it, the tree would produce golden apples again. But they don't know that, of course." He chuckled at all the misery he had caused and closed his eyes again.

Again, Hansel waited until the Devil's breathing was nice and even, and a third time he plucked out a golden hair.

"Father above and Me below!" screamed the Devil, sitting up. "Don't tell me! You had another bad dream!"

"Yes!" Hansel said. "I'm so sorry!"

The Devil settled himself back in Hansel's lap. "I'm getting sick of this," he said. "Tell me the dream, but if you pull my hair again, I'll put you out there with the sinners."

"I dreamed there was a poor ferryman," Hansel said, "who had been in his boat for seven years, and couldn't leave, no matter how hard he tried."

"Aha! The old fool!" said the Devil. "All he has to do is hand his paddle off to someone else, and he'll be free, and *they'll* be stuck there for the rest of time. But he doesn't know that, of course." He chuckled at the agony he had caused, and said, "Now don't wake me again, or you'll be sorry."

He was just settling into a nice, peaceful sleep, with Hansel holding the three golden hairs in his hand and shaking like a leaf, when a scream pierced the house. The Devil sat up. "What in Hell was that?" he shouted.

"It sounds like someone in the attic!" Hansel said. "Has one of the sinners escaped?"

"We'll soon find out!" the Devil cried, and he leaped to his feet and ran up the stairs. As soon as he was out of sight, Hansel jumped up, threw the wig and dress off, and banged out of the door of the house. He turned for the doors of Hell and broke into a run, gripping the three golden hairs tightly.

After a while he glanced briefly over his shoulder. To his surprise, he discovered that the fire and the pits and the demons with the pitchforks had disappeared. All he saw now were poor sinners, writhing on the floor of a great cave, screaming in sorrow and remorse for all the pain they had caused. Holding the three golden hairs, he knew that he was seeing the truth—Hell as it really was.

He arrived at the great black doors. As he laid his hands on them they swung open, and he stood blinking in the daylight.

The old man, who had been sitting on the ground just outside all this time, leaped to his feet. "You're out!" he cried. "Hallelujah!" And then he said, "Why are you wearing makeup?"

But just at that moment, a terrible cry echoed from the depths of Hell—the unmistakable, blood-chilling, hair-raising, stomach-turning cry of the Devil.

"Run!" Hansel cried. And they did. They sprinted over the dusty ground away from the black doors of Hell. Glancing over his shoulder, Hansel saw the furious Devil, galloping across the turf behind them. For, you see, outside of Hell the Devil has no power over those who are not already damned, and so he had to chase them on foot.

Still, he was faster than the young boy and the old man. He wasn't far behind them when they arrived at the river. They jumped in the ferryman's boat and shoved it off from shore.

"Did you discover how to free me?" the ferryman said.

"I did," Hansel replied, "but take us across first! Look! The Devil's after us!"

So the ferryman rowed with all of his might. When Hansel and the old man got out of the boat, Hansel told the ferryman what to do.

The ferryman returned to the other shore, where the Devil was waiting impatiently. "After those two! Now!" the Devil commanded, hopping in. So the ferryman started off. But he paddled as slowly as he possibly could. "Hurry!" screamed the Devil. "They're getting away!"

But the ferryman said, "I can't go any faster. The current's too strong for me."

"Oh, to Hell with that!" the Devil cried, and grabbed the paddle from the ferryman's hands. He paddled them across the river in the blink of an eye, but when they reached the other shore, the ferryman hopped out, and the Devil found that he was stuck fast. He bellowed and hollered and screamed and cried, but no amount of protest would set him free.

The ferryman then set about making a little sign with some clay and a piece of slate to explain the situation to all who came by so that no one would accidentally free the Devil. He adorned it with flowers and smiling angels. The Devil fumed. But he was stuck in that boat for many years to come.

The old man laughed and laughed to see the Devil in the little ferryboat, struggling to get out, and Hansel laughed, too, and wiped the grandmother's makeup from his face. And they began to walk back toward the walled cities to tell the people how to break the Devil's curses.

But after walking just a little way, the old man stumbled. Hansel caught him, and they began to walk again. But a little while on he stumbled a second time, and this time he fell to the ground.

Hansel tried to help him to his feet, but the old man was breathing hard. "Let me lie here a moment," he said. The race with the Devil had taken its toll on his ancient body. So Hansel sat beside the man and, because the old man asked him to, told him all about his time in Hell, and what he had done to escape.

The old man laughed when Hansel told him of dressing up like the Devil's grandmother, and laughed some more when Hansel described singing the Devil to sleep. But soon the old man's laughter became a fit of coughing. He put his head back in the grass and tried to breathe calmly. After a while, he took Hansel's hand.

"I can go no farther," he said. Making the words was an effort for him. "Stay beside me, Hansel. Don't run from me now."

"Why would I run from you?" Hansel asked.

"You ran from your parents because of me," the old man said.

Hansel didn't know what he was talking about. "I ran away because my father cut off my head," he said. "And how did you know I ran away?"

"Who *told* him to cut off your head?" The old man's voice was weak.

"A statu—" Hansel began. He stopped. He gazed at the man's ancient, wrinkled face. Then, after a moment, he said, "You did."

"I did," said Faithful Johannes. He tried to raise himself to sit, but his face twisted with pain and he gave up. "I've been seeking you and your sister all these years. Now I've found you, and I'm dying."

They sat there, the old man and the young boy, on a patch of grass by the side of the road. The clouds passed overhead, the late autumn sun dipped low in the western sky, and the crickets took up their song.

And then, because he thought about it every morning when he woke up and every evening when he lay down, Hansel said, "Tell me about my parents."

Johannes smiled sadly. "They cursed themselves, Hansel, for what they did to you two. They were foolish—foolish!" He coughed angrily. "They see their foolishness now. And so do I. Faithfulness is important. Under-standing is important. But nothing is as precious as children. Nothing."

The cricket-song enveloped them once again. A flock of swallows swooped overhead, their little brown bodies framed by the pink sky. Hansel thought of the seven brothers.

"I don't want to go home," he said. "Don't make me." He suddenly felt like a very little child again.

"I understand," Johannes said.

"No, you don't."

Johannes sighed. "Hansel, I do." And then he began to tell the boy a story. It started with a dying king and a young prince and a beautiful princess who lived across the sea. The prince became a king, and he convinced the beautiful princess to be his wife (Johannes left out the whole *stealing* thing, for his strength was low; and besides, it was pretty embarrassing). Then he told of three ravens and three prophecies. And a faithful servant, who risked his very life.

"I loved this young king and his bride," Johannes said. "And I thought, perhaps, that they would keep their faith with me. That they would under-stand." And he told Hansel of the chestnut stallion and the golden dress and the wedding dance. And of carrying the new queen to the highest turret. And of what he did there. And of the pyre, and all the rest.

Hansel stared at the grass as the shadows grew and the sky turned from pale blue to orange and pink. Locusts hummed. "Can you ever forgive them?" Hansel asked softly.

"I did better than forgive them," Johannes said. "I understood them."

"I understand too, but—"

"Not in the new sense of the word," Johannes interrupted. "In the *old* sense. The ancient sense. I under-stood." He paused and collected his breath. "I planted my feet beneath them and took upon my shoulders their burden—their choice, their mistake, and their pain. Yes, I understood them; but I also *under-stood* them.

"In the last moment, before I turned to stone, your parents understood what I had done for them. But only on that terrible day, when they cut off your heads, did they under-stand me; only on that day were they willing to stand beneath me and take on my burden. It was that that brought me back to life.

"So I understand you, Hansel. And I under-stand you. But that, unfortunately, isn't good enough. It's not from me that you need under-standing."

Suddenly, a terrible fit of coughing took the ancient man. He doubled up, and Hansel held him by the shoulders. After a while, he was able to lie back down. There was blood on his lips, and on his face.

"Listen to me now, Hansel. Listen well." Johannes's voice was low and hard to hear. Hansel put his head right up by Johannes's mouth—much as Johannes had done for Hansel's grandfather, many years before. "There is an evil thing," Johannes said. "An evil thing in the kingdom. Because of their weakness, and their sadness, a dragon has come has come to the Kingdom of Grimm."

Hansel tried to sit up, but the old man's grip was iron on his sleeve. "Listen to me. The dragon has taken possession of one of the people. It lives inside him, like a disease."

"Who?"

But Johannes motioned for him to be quiet. Speaking was now a great struggle. "You must kill it. You and Gretel."

"Why us?"

"Because there is a time when a kingdom needs its children," Johannes said.

Hansel sat quietly under the pink and purpling sky. He thought of the kingdom, and his parents, and of the years that had passed. He thought of the pain he felt, the heavy burden of pain. He thought of what Johannes had said about understanding.

"We'll go to them," Hansel said. "I'll find Gretel, and we will save our parents and their kingdom."

The old man smiled. He reached out and took Hansel's hand. They sat together as the light faded, and the sky went from blue to deep purple to black. Hansel stared up at the stars as they winked into being—one, two, three, four . . .

He turned back to Johannes. The old man's eyes stared upward, but he was not seeing. Hansel waved a hand before his face, and then touched his neck. Johannes was dead.

HANSEL and GRETEL
and the
Broken Kingdom

*O*nce upon a time, a little girl stopped into a tavern that stood along the side of a road. She shook her traveling cloak as she stood in the doorway, and wet slush fell from it to the rough wooden floor. Outside, the last gasps of winter tossed the branches of the trees, and the road was a mess of water and ice.

Gretel sat down near the fireplace, and the tavern owner brought her warm milk in a pewter mug. She paid for it from the pouch the villagers had given her when she'd left them. Then she sat and stared gloomily at the logs in the hearth, their ashy gray outsides spreading, deadening the fire inside. She knew just what that felt like.

Months. Months on the road as the leaves had turned from

red to brown and then had fallen. As the snow had begun to drift down from the gray sky—softly at first, and then heavily, piling onto the frozen road in front of Gretel in white, shifting mounds. She had wrapped her cloak around her tightly, but still the cold seeped into her skin, down to her bones. From time to time her feet would slide out from beneath her as she walked, sending her sprawling into a mound of fluffy snow—or worse, a deep puddle of icy water. She walked without knowing where she was going, and, more and more every day, without caring where she was going, either.

She had lived with parents and without. In homes and in the wild. Nothing was good.

Oh, yes. And Hansel was dead.

She laid her little golden head beside the pewter mug on the worn tavern table. The table was sticky from spilled drinks. Gretel didn't care. She closed her eyes.

There was a bang, and the door of the inn swung open. Gretel raised her head. A man stood in the doorway. "It's back!" he cried, his voice cracking with fear. "It's back . . ."

The people of the tavern all rose to their feet at once.

"Kindheitburg is gone!" the man wailed.

Cries rose up from all around. A few people pushed past

the man out the tavern door and onto the slushy road, and began to run.

"What do you mean, gone?" someone demanded.

"It's all gone," the man in the doorway said. "The houses, Meister Beck's, the bakery, Frau Hopper's . . ."

"The people?"

"I don't know. But there were bodies." He shook his head. "Many bodies."

The room seemed to groan all together. Some people sat down. Others covered their faces.

"I was out on the hill above town," the man said. "I saw it circling, circling over the village. I would have run back to warn them, but there wasn't time. Besides, I had to stay with this one." From behind the man's leg, a tiny girl peeked out. She was hiding her face in her hands, but you could tell that her cheeks were stained with dirt and the lines of dried tears.

The man went on. "It circled three or four times. I could hear people shouting. Then it banked and began to descend. It swept in on Frau Hopper's house—the big stone one. Tore half the building off. I saw somebody—maybe Frau Hopper—fly through the air about a hundred yards. And then crash to the ground." The man shuddered.

"And after that?" someone asked.

The man shuddered again but said no more. An elderly man nearby guided him to a seat and brought him a drink. He put his head in his hands. A large, heavyset woman came from behind the bar and lifted the little girl up and cradled her and took her up some stairs in the back.

When the door was closed behind the woman with the little girl, the somber tavern suddenly erupted with anxious voices. Gretel tried to make sense of it, but they spoke all together, and too loudly. What were they talking about? What had done this thing? Then, gradually, she was able to pick up one word that was being repeated over and over in the din: *dragon.*

Gretel was standing near three people—two men, a tall one and a bearded one, and a woman whose back was toward Gretel.

"They say it's human," said the bearded man.

"Half-human," replied the tall one. "And half-dragon, of course."

"My priest said it was once a man, but now he's possessed by a dragon-spirit," said the woman.

"It would have to be a devil-man, to be possessed by a dragon."

"No," the woman replied. "The priest said no. He said a sad soul. A desperate soul. That's what he said."

"Yes, I heard that, too," the bearded man agreed.

The tall one rubbed his stubbly chin. "They killed that man over in Walden. They thought he was the dragon."

"Guess he wasn't, then."

"Guess not. He had children, too."

"They killed six brothers over in Hamelstatt," said the woman.

"No, that's a rumor."

"It isn't. My cousin saw it happen."

"Terrible," said the man with the beard.

"Terrible," said the tall man.

"Terrible," said the woman.

"Excuse me," said Gretel. She was standing at the woman's elbow. The woman didn't seem to hear her. Gretel tugged at the woman's sleeve. "Excuse me," she said again. The woman turned around. Her face was pale, her hair hung loose and limp, and her light eyes were circled with black.

"What is it?" the woman said.

"What kingdom is this?" Gretel asked.

"Grimm," the woman said. "The Kingdom of Grimm."

"Or it was," the bearded man said ruefully. "Now it's the ruins of Grimm."

"Where are you looking for?" said the tall man.

Gretel's throat felt thick. "Do the king and queen have any children?" she asked quietly.

The woman looked at the men, and then back at her. "Did once. Twins. A boy and a girl. But they were lost, poor darlings. Disappeared in the night."

"Just before the dragon came," the man with the beard added.

"That's right. Just before," agreed the tall one. "But where are you trying to get to?"

Gretel hesitated. "I . . . I'm not sure," she replied. She thanked the group and walked to the door of the inn. Two men were standing beside it, arguing about the dragon. She stood behind them, half waiting, half thinking. At length, one noticed her, nudged the other, and they both turned to her.

"Can I help you, dearie?"

She bit her bottom lip. After a moment, she asked, "Which way is the castle?" She said it as if she wasn't sure she wanted to know.

The men pointed with blunt workmen's fingers.

Gretel nodded silently and stepped out the door of the tavern onto the road. She looked in the direction they had pointed.

Even the road looked rough, painful.

She looked the other way.

Hansel traveled down the wet, icy roads, a solitary boy with charcoal eyes and curly black hair laden with flakes of snow.

Behind him followed two obedient oxen, pulling two positively enormous carts.

The first cart was filled with golden apples—a thousand of them—round and firm and cool. Golden as in made of gold, of course. Not Golden Delicious. Golden Expensive. The second cart was filled with barrels of wine—barrels stacked so high that they tottered and creaked with every turning in the road. There was enough wine in those barrels to keep a whole village in drink for a whole year.

The apples and the wine and the carts and the oxen were all gifts from the two villages, of course. You see, after burying Johannes and making a little headstone for him—*Faithful* was all it said—Hansel had gone on to the village of the golden apples, where he told them of the mouse gnawing at the roots of their tree. They killed it, and the apples began to grow immediately, and so they gave him as a gift the thousand golden apples and the cart and the quiet, obedient, incredibly large ox. Next he had gone to the village of the wine, where he told them of the frog stopping up their fountain. Once they had killed it, the wine began to flow again, and they gave Hansel as a gift the barrels of wine, the cart, and another quiet, obedient, incredibly large ox.

He named the oxen Ivy and Betty—which is strange, because oxen are boys.

———

That doesn't come into the story much. I just thought I'd tell you.

So Hansel, having bested the Devil, and saved the two villages, and now leading a fortune in wine and gold, set out for the Kingdom of Grimm. It wasn't hard to get directions, either. Everyone could point you toward a kingdom where a dragon was.

But Hansel's progress was slow. For he stopped at every village, every hamlet, every house and hovel he passed along the way, to ask if they had seen or heard anything of his sister, Gretel. But no one had.

"You mean Gretel, the old woman?"

"No, my sister."

"Gretel, my sister's baby?"

"No, *my* sister. And she's not a baby."

"I have a goat named Gretel."

"No!"

He may have had a fortune in gold and wine behind him, and two obedient oxen to follow him wherever he went, but Hansel's heart was as black and heavy as it had ever been, and his feet dragged in the mud and the ice. Without his sister, he did not want to go home. Or face a dragon. Or face his parents.

Gretel stood at the door of the tavern, staring down the road. Coming toward her were two enormous oxcarts, each capped, like miniature mountains, with snow. Walking out in front of them was someone with dark hair—a small, dejected someone, whose feet dragged as he walked. There was something about the someone that made Gretel want to wait for him.

As the carts drew nearer, her heart caught in her throat. With her fine, ocean-blue eyes, Gretel could now make out the someone's face.

She cried aloud and tore off for him down the road.

As Hansel drew closer to the kingdom, he seemed to see Gretel everywhere. In bakeries. In upstairs windows. Going into out-houses (which resulted in some pretty embarrassing moments, as you can imagine). Just up ahead, there was a girl standing at the doorway of a tavern, and, had he not known he was just seeing things, he would have sworn that that girl was Gretel, too.

Then the girl was no longer standing at the door of the tavern. She was sprinting toward him, her long blond hair flying out behind her. Hansel blinked. He stopped dragging his feet. He ran.

Hansel and Gretel came together like two magnets meeting, like meteors that have been screaming through space toward this one moment of collision. They met in the middle with a bang, and instantly their feet went out from under them on the slick roadway. They landed, hard, in a puddle of icy mud.

They stared at each other, sitting in the puddle.

Lost and then found.

Dead and then alive.

Covered in mud.

Sitting on their behinds in three inches of filthy water.

And they began to laugh. They threw their arms around each other and laughed until tears streamed down their faces. They sat, freezing, muddy, in a puddle in the middle of the road, with the gray sky overhead, and their parents' castle waiting just a few miles away. They sat there and held each other until their arms ached.

"Where have you been?" Hansel asked as they pulled themselves out of the puddle.

"How are you alive?" Gretel asked at just the same moment.

So they climbed up on an oxcart and told each other about every single thing that had happened since the day of the hunt in the Lebenwald—and some things twice.

And as they talked and laughed and gasped and talked some more, Ivy and Betty drew them closer and closer to home.

Hansel and Gretel are coming to the hardest part now.

It's true that they've been nearly eaten by a cannibalistic baker woman; and they've talked to the fiery sun and to the child-eating moon and to the kind stars; and they've journeyed to the Crystal Mountain; and that Gretel has cut off her own finger, and caused somebody to be boiled alive; and that Hansel has been turned into a beast and been shot and skinned and gambled away; and that he went to Hell and dressed up like the Devil's grandmother; and that he's been chased by the Devil himself and has held an old man's hand as he died.

It's true they've done all those things.

But sometimes, coming home is the hardest thing of all.

Soon Hansel and Gretel found themselves in the heart of the Kingdom of Grimm, driving through towns that still lived in their earliest memories. As they looked around, their stomachs began to twist into knots.

Some of the towns looked just as they remembered them, as if memories of home could be modeled in wood and brick.

But other towns—other memories of home—had been razed to the ground. Houses were torn apart, with their roofs and walls scattered and broken. Shops were burned, eviscerated, empty. Dead animals lay in the street, their bloated bellies stiffening as flies walked carefully across the surface of their eyeballs.

"The dragon," Gretel murmured.

Hansel nodded and stared.

As they passed through one gutted town, the door on the wreckage of a house began to move. Its hinges groaned angrily. Hansel leaned close to Gretel. She took his hand. Then, from the darkness, a head emerged.

It was a child. He was very small—the size of the child Gretel had seen in the tavern. He was followed by an older child, a girl, and then a still-older girl.

"Come out," the eldest said. "Look."

From behind them emerged their parents. The whole family was dirty, emaciated, with ragged clothes and frightened eyes.

Gretel said, "This is not good."

"No," Hansel said. "It isn't."

Suddenly, Gretel jumped down from the cart and ran around to the back. "I'm going to give them an apple," she shouted to Hansel.

The family heard this, and the father and mother and three

children all came out to the cart. "You have apples?" the father said.

"Not the kind you eat," Gretel told him. "But this might help you." And she reached under the canvas tarp, took out an apple, and gave it to them.

"It's golden!" the children cried, and the parents' eyes grew wide with wonder. But the eldest of the children, who was a few years older than Gretel, stared at her.

"She looks like the princess," the girl said.

The family stopped marveling at the apple and looked at Gretel again. "She does . . ." the father said. And then, tentatively, he said, "Your Highness?" Gretel blushed.

The eldest child had run around to the front of the cart. "And the prince!" she shouted.

All the rest of their journey home, the family ran ahead of the oxcart, cheering and shouting for all to hear, "The prince and princess are home! The prince and princess are home!"

People began to come out of their houses. Slowly at first, peering fearfully around their doors. But when they saw the two children sitting atop the oxcarts, and the family walking before them, shouting at the top of their lungs, the villagers' frightened faces gradually lifted, and they came out into the warming sun to walk behind the oxcarts and cheer.

Soon Hansel and Gretel had a train of followers a thousand people strong, and still they gathered more as they went.

They looked around them at the cheering, shouting, laughing people. Never had they felt so special, so important. They were just children, after all.

Word of their arrival ran ahead of them. It did not take long for it to reach the king and queen at the castle.

At first, neither king nor queen believed it. There had been rumors of the children's return before. But as the reports were confirmed, and confirmed again, and then again, king and queen, Father and Mother, grew too agitated to wait any longer. They rushed to the great gate of the castle with pounding hearts and clasped hands.

As the castle came into view, with its tall turrets and broad porticoes, Gretel took her brother's arm. She held it so tight it began to hurt. He looked at her. Her face was lined with worry. "You don't think . . ." She stopped. She began again. "They won't do—what they did—again?"

Slowly, Hansel shook his head. "No," he said. And he repeated all Faithful Johannes had told him. "They miss us," he concluded. "And they're very sorry."

Gretel nodded. Hansel found her hand and held it.

When the oxcarts were only a hundred feet from the gate, Hansel and Gretel got down. Their mother and father ran toward them, arms outstretched. Hansel and Gretel stood and watched them come. They did not reach out their arms, but, when their parents reached them, they allowed themselves to be lifted up and held.

"I am so sorry," was the first thing their father said.

"I am so sorry," was the first thing their mother said.

And they kissed their children's cheeks and wet them with their tears and held them tight. They told the servants to care for the oxen and put the canvas-covered carts in the royal stables, and then they brought Hansel and Gretel into the castle, where they washed them and fed them.

At last, the whole family sat before a glowing hearth in the private wing of the castle. The shadows of flames danced on their faces. "Tell us everything," the queen said, her face beaming. "Where have you been? What have you done? How did you find your way home?"

Hansel and Gretel looked at their parents, and then at each other. They shrugged. Then they looked at the thick red rug on the floor.

It will happen to you, dear reader, at some point in your life. You will face a moment very much like the one Hansel and Gretel are facing right now.

In this moment, you will look at your parents and realize that—no matter what it sounds like they are saying—they are actually asking you for forgiveness. This is a very painful moment. You see, all of your life you've been asking for forgiveness from them. From the age you can talk you are apologizing for breaking this, forgetting that, hitting him, locking her in the garage, and so on. So, having them ask *you* for forgiveness probably sounds pretty good.

But when this moment comes, you will probably be in a *lot* of pain. And you probably will not want to forgive them.

In which case, what, you might ask, should you do?

Well, you could yell at them, and tell them about all the ways they've hurt you. This is a good thing to do once, because—believe me—they need to know. But this is the first step on the road to forgiveness. What if you're not even ready for that?

You could pretend to forgive them. This I would not recommend. It's sort of like sweeping broken glass under the carpet; the floor still isn't clean, and somebody's going to end up with a bloody sock.

Finally, if you don't want to forgive them, and you don't want to fake it, you can always go with Ol' Reliable: Changing the subject.

After a moment, Hansel said, "What about the dragon?"

And Gretel said, "Yes, tell us about that."

The king and queen exchanged an anxious look. Their children—they were still children, were they not?—seemed so different from the little ones that had frolicked at the foot of their bed on the very day they'd been lost. These two were so serious, so silent, so distant. But the king and queen agreed with merely a look, as only parents can, that it was best to give them their time and their space. And so they told Hansel and Gretel all about the dragon.

After the children had disappeared, the king explained, he had gone out every day to look for them. At first, he had taken hunting parties with him. But soon he had become so distraught that he insisted on going out alone. He described pushing through the wet leaves of early spring, persevering through the hailstorms of March and the thunderstorms of April to find them. But he never turned up a single trace of them. And it was on one of these days, when he was far from the castle, that the dragon had come.

It began by circling in the sky, the queen said. The villagers below ran in a panic every which way, unsure where to go or what to do. When the dragon dove that first time, it screamed, and it was said that villages two miles away heard it. At the end of that first day, one town was utterly gone, and hundreds and hundreds of people were dead.

Hansel said, "What does it look like?" The queen shuddered.

"It's hideous. Smooth black skin, like a snake's. Eyes that are golden—with no whites or pupils at all. Its wings are so thin, you can see through them. And each of its talons and teeth look like long, sharp obsidian shards."

When the king came home that first night and saw what had happened, he assembled an army, and they rode out to meet the beast. But they could not find it. Every day for a week they rode around looking for the dragon. But never would it show its face. Then, one day, the army was under the direction of the captain of the guards, for the king had been taken ill. That day, the king said bitterly, the dragon had come, and it destroyed the army completely. Now there were few soldiers left in the kingdom, and fewer still who would face the dragon. There had been nothing anyone could do for a long time now—except watch the dragon tear the kingdom apart.

Gretel's brow furrowed. "Well," she said at last, "Hansel and I will come up with something."

The king and queen smiled at her as if she were a very little child, and then they smiled at each other. "That's very brave of you," the queen said gently. "But we're just happy to have you home. You don't have to worry yourself about the dragon, dear."

Gretel stood up. Her eyes were almost level with those of her seated parents. Almost.

"Has either of you ever had to cut off your own finger?" she asked.

They stared at her. She raised her left hand to show them. They gasped.

"No? How about killing people? How many people have you killed?"

"Killed?" her father said.

"Yes. Besides me and Hansel."

The king's face grew red, and his voice quiet. "None, honey. Why?"

"Well, we have. Two," Gretel said.

Hansel stood up beside her. "Has either of you been to Hell?" he asked.

"What?" his parents cried.

"Been tortured by demons?" Hansel added.

They shook their heads and stared at their children.

He gave them one last chance. "Had the Devil's head in your lap?"

Neither replied.

"Then I think you'd better leave this to us," Gretel said. And the two children went back to their room to talk things over.

An hour later they returned. "So," Hansel said, "dragons love treasure, right?"

"At least in storybooks," Gretel added.

Their parents looked at each other and shrugged. "I guess," the king replied.

"Okay, let's say they do," Hansel said. "We have a cartload of golden apples in the stable right now."

His mother's eyes grew wide. "You do?"

"How on earth did you get that?" the king asked.

"We'll explain later," Gretel said impatiently. "Are you listening?"

The king and queen nodded sheepishly.

"Okay, so we take the cart of apples out to a clearing in the forest," Hansel said.

"We open it up," Gretel cut in, "so the dragon can see it. Hopefully, he'll be attracted to the gold."

"We'll have to raise an army. They'll be hiding in the trees all around," Hansel said. "With bows and arrows."

"And swords and axes," Gretel added.

"And when the dragon is distracted by the apples, the archers will fire at it from the cover of the trees. It won't know where the arrows are coming from, and it will be confused and, hopefully, wounded."

"And that's when everyone else will run out and attack it," Gretel concluded.

Slowly, the queen began to nod. "That's not a bad plan," she said. She turned to the king.

Well, the king tried to find some fault or other, because that's what fathers do. "Raising an army," he said. "That will be difficult. Our people don't want to fight anymore. They're afraid."

"We have to try," Hansel said.

"It may not work," Gretel agreed. "But it's better than doing nothing."

After a few more perfunctory objections, their father finally had to admit that, indeed, it sounded like a pretty good plan.

The queen, blushing a little, said, "Do you need *all* the apples for the plan? If so, I understand, of course . . . I just . . ."

The king smiled. "Your mother would like an apple," he said. "She's always had a passion for gold. That's how we met, you know."

"I heard," Gretel said. "You *stole* her."

"I did not!" the king said.

"Admit it, darling," the queen laughed. "You sort of did."

"You *stole* Mother?" Hansel asked.

"Well, yes . . . I . . . I suppose . . . I sort of did."

The king laughed at himself, and the queen laughed some more. Hansel and Gretel began to smile. It was the first crack in their armor their parents had yet seen. The king and the queen, laughing and tearful, reached out their arms to their children.

But with that, the children's smiles died away. After a moment, the king and queen lowered their arms.

Gretel whispered, "We have to go to bed now. It's late, and we have a lot to do tomorrow."

Hansel stood without moving for a moment. Then he said, "Yes. That's true."

And the two children turned away from their parents and went upstairs to bed.

"I feel like something is pressing down on my chest," Gretel said, lying in her bed that night, her eyes wide open. "Something heavy and sharp and painful. I've felt it for a long, long time now."

"Since we left," Hansel said, nodding in the darkness.

"Since just before we left," Gretel corrected him. There was silence. Then she said, "It's been getting worse recently. It's never been so bad as it is right now. I feel like I can barely breathe."

"I know."

"I just want to take it and throw it off of me. Make someone else feel it and hold it and carry it for a while."

The beds creaked and settled beneath them. They had been empty for a long time. At last, Hansel said, "Not just *someone* else."

"No," Gretel agreed. "Not just *someone* else."

HANSEL and GRETEL
and
the Dragon

*O*nce upon a time, on a bright but sunless morning, Hansel and Gretel stood in the middle of the town of Wachsend's tiny central square. Actually, it wasn't even a square. It was more like a grassy hole between the tavern and the bakery. Hansel and Gretel wore their finest, most regal clothes, and, so that all could see them, they stood on a table that had been brought out from the tavern.

The people of Wachsend gathered around the black-haired prince and the golden-blond princess and peered at them wonderingly, expectantly. This was the strangest thing to have happened in their little town in anyone's memory. Not only was it unheard of for royalty to pay them a visit, unless in some grand procession that was just passing through (Hansel and Gretel had come alone—*alone*!), but the prince and princess had been the talk of the kingdom since their return. To see them? Here? Well, you can imagine that no self-respecting Wachsender would miss it.

So they gathered in the grassy square, beneath birds that sang in the bare branches of the trees, and waited to hear what had brought the young prince and princess to their town.

Hansel shifted uneasily from foot to foot as he looked at the expectant faces before him. Wachsend had been lucky so far. The dragon had not yet visited. But nonetheless the people were thin, from the lean times the dragon had brought to the kingdom. And they looked afraid. There seemed to be fear lingering at the corners of their mouths; a few even glanced up at the sky periodically. Hansel didn't have to ask what they were looking for.

Gretel saw all this, too. And then she began to speak to the people of Wachsend.

She told them she knew they were scared. She told them that she was scared, too. She told them that fear would not save them from the dragon. She told them that only courage would save them. They must fight it, she said. *They must fight it.*

Gretel spoke, and the people of Wachsend—grown men and women—listened to her. Not a single villager spoke, not a single villager moved. When she had finished, every person was totally still.

And then someone shouted, "What?"

"What did she say?" cried someone else.

Gretel looked confused. Had they not been able to hear her?

"She must be out of her mind!" another called.

"She's crazy!"

"Is that child talking to *us*?"

They had heard her. Gretel turned red. Hansel cut in. "If we do nothing," he said, "the dragon will destroy the entire kingdom. We'll die! We might as well fight it!"

"Join us!" Gretel called desperately. "Do something that you will be able to tell your children, and your children's children! Join us and fight the dragon!"

A single person cheered.

"We need you all!" Hansel said, taking encouragement from this one enthusiast. "Men and women, veterans and volunteers! Anyone who can shoot an arrow or hold a weapon! We need you all!"

"I volunteer!" that single person called.

"Yes!" cried another. "Let's fight it!"

The crowd began to hum with talk. Hansel and Gretel looked at each other. It was working. It was working.

"Are you crazy?" suddenly rang out above the hum and din.

Heads turned. Hansel and Gretel looked around for the source of the cry.

"You people must be nuts!"

It was a tall man, thin but muscular, with a bald head and a boxer's nose. He stood near the back of the group.

"What do you think you're doing?" he went on. "Have you seen the dragon? Have you fought it before? It will kill you. It will kill all of you!"

"Shut up!" someone cried.

"We've got to do something!" someone else called out.

"Die? Is that what we have to do?" He paused. No one responded. "I've seen this beast. I was there when we fought it the first time. You can't beat it. Arrows practically bounce off of it. It can kill four people at once, one with each of its four feet. And look at *them*!" he said, gesturing at Hansel and Gretel. "They're children! Children! You're going to follow *children* into battle against a *dragon*? Are you all out of your minds?!"

There was a pause. The subjects of Wachsend turned to hear the prince and princess's reply. Hansel was red in the face. Gretel was pale. They stared out over their subjects. All was quiet. The children opened their mouths. But neither had anything to say.

"Ridiculous!" the bald man cried. And he turned his back on

Hansel and Gretel and walked into the tavern. The door closed with a slam.

"Wait!" Hansel shouted. "Wait!"

But suddenly, people were dispersing, heading to the tavern or back to their homes.

"Would you rather die in a tavern or on a field of battle?" Hansel cried.

"A tavern!" someone shouted, and a few others laughed. More Wachsenders turned their backs on Hansel and Gretel.

"Would you rather die having done nothing or having tried?"

"Nothing!" someone called. But those who would have laughed were gone now. The remaining villagers were silent.

"Will you follow us to fight the dragon?" Hansel asked.

More silence.

"If you will," Gretel said, "meet us at the castle in three days' time. Bring your weapon of choice. And," she added, with as much strength as she had left, "bring your courage!"

As Hansel and Gretel made their way out of Wachsend, Hansel turned to his sister. "Well," he said, "that went terribly."

"Yes, it did," she replied. They walked a little farther. Then she asked, "Ready to do it again?"

He sighed. "I guess so."

And they set off for the next town.

———

Three days later, Hansel and Gretel waited in the castle courtyard. Scattered around it were groups of volunteers. Small groups. No more than a handful apiece.

"It's early yet," Gretel said. "More will come."

Hansel wrung his sweaty hands. "I suppose," he said.

The recruitment had been brutal. Town after town. "Are you crazy?" "What do you think you're going to do?" "You're just children!" "They're just children!" "You're going to follow children into battle?" There had been some who seemed ready to fight. A few. But most grew silent and wary when they heard they were expected to follow Hansel and Gretel—little Hansel and Gretel—to war.

But as the hours went by in the castle courtyard, people came. Raw recruits, carrying hunting bows and even pitchforks, made their way through the great gates. But there were also groups that were obviously veterans—men with thick necks and wooden shields and shining swords. There were women, too. Archers, mostly; but also women carrying swords and spears. One had a rake.

"We'd better get that one something proper to fight with," Hansel said, pointing.

Gretel chuckled and nodded.

By late afternoon, the children felt better. Before them stood some five hundred soldiers. It wasn't an enormous group. And it certainly wasn't a pretty group. But it would do. It would do.

The children's chests swelled. They had done it. They had raised an army.

The king and queen, however, were suddenly no longer so keen on Hansel and Gretel's plan.

"Wait, *you're* going out?" said the queen when the children came before them that night. "You never said anything about *you* going out."

"They're *not* going out," the king said. "I will not allow it."

The queen looked at the two children as they stood before her, stone-faced and armed. "Please," she said, "we've already lost you once. We couldn't stand losing you again. Please. My children." She began, softly, to cry.

Their father came and knelt before them and took each one by the hand. "Please, my dears," he said. "Understand. You are children. Why can't you send someone else out in your stead?"

"Father," Gretel said, "maybe you should try to understand that yourself."

She and Hansel drew their hands away. Their mother began to cry louder.

Hansel and Gretel went to the stable to ready the oxcart with the golden apples. The apples were held securely under a canvas tarp and—except for the one apple they had given to the poor family, and the other they had given to their mother—they were all there.

As Gretel hitched the cart up to Betty, Hansel looked under the cover of the other. "What about the wine?" he said. "Maybe we could get the dragon drunk." Gretel smiled. But he said, "Really. Why not?"

"It couldn't hurt, I guess," Gretel said. So they hitched up Ivy, too.

When the sky was black and dotted with stars and the moon was just beginning to creep above the horizon, big and round and white, the two children led the oxcarts out into the darkness. Hansel and Gretel looked back over their shoulders with pride. Behind them followed their army.

They led them down a road to a large wood that stood not far from the castle. As they approached, the army began to whisper and point. The ground at the wood's edge seemed to glow, as if the moon was reflected by the very soil. It shimmered and sparkled, an earthbound Milky Way. *Was it magic?* the soldiers asked one another. *Or a sign from the dragon?*

ADAM GIDWITZ

But Hansel and Gretel confidently followed the path of white pebbles that they had scattered on the forest floor the day before, leading their army deep into the wood, to a large, grassy clearing.

Here, for the first time, Hansel and Gretel told the army their plan. They would all stay in hiding until the dragon came for the bait. When it came—*if* it came—they would wait until it was distracted by the contents of the oxcarts. Then, when it was least ready to defend itself, they would spring out of their hiding places and attack.

"You have every right to be afraid," Gretel told them. "The dragon is big. The dragon is strong. The dragon has divided our families and taken our children and stolen our childhoods.

"But that is no reason to cower. Until we stand up to him, our lives will remain shattered, our hearts will remain divided against themselves, our heads will remain severed from our bodies."

The moon was white and bright behind Gretel. Hansel stared at her. He didn't quite understand what she was talking about.

"But we will soon be healed," she went on. "We will be healed. There will be blood first. But then there will be tears of joy.

"For our kingdom!" she shouted.

"And our families!" Hansel cried.

"And our children!" they said together.

The soldiers repeated their cry. In the silence that followed, all could hear the word *children* echoing off the thick trees and then away through the black wood.

Gretel readied the oxcarts in the clearing. In the moonlight, the apples glowed golden, as if they possessed some fairy magic. Hansel unharnessed Ivy and Betty from the carts and tried to shoo them off. But the two oxen took to cropping grass nearby. Someone had to draw them by their halters far off into the woods, as far as possible from the field of battle.

Don't worry. Ivy and Betty will be fine.

(I just wish I could say the same for everyone else.)

Leaving both carts out in the clearing, the two children retreated to the cover of trees to watch, and wait.

The forest made sounds. Branches creaking. Leaves whispering to one another. Bats flapping between trees, looking for prey. Hansel plucked the grass at his feet. Gretel fingered a small dagger strapped to her belt. The volunteer soldiers began shifting uneasily. One did not venture into a wood at night. Especially not when there was a dragon about. Sword handles became slick with sweat, bowstrings were pulled back and released, pulled back and released. An owl hooted. Far off, they could hear its great wings beating against the air.

No.

They were not the wings of an owl. The beats were too far apart. Too deep and distant. Hansel and Gretel peered out from under the cover of branches and leaves, but they could see nothing against the black, starry sky.

And then there it was. In front of the moon. The long, thin silhouette of the dragon, its wings resting on the currents of night air.

Its body was narrow, its four feet were tucked up underneath it, its long tail trailed out behind. Its wings were so thin that the moonlight shone through them. Stifled gasps arose from those who had never seen it. It was disgusting. It was enormous. From below, one could see the outline of its head, broad and viperlike. It looked nothing like the dragons in storybooks.

Not even the dragon on the cover of this book, dear reader.

Go ahead, take a look.

That dragon, you see, was designed to alert you to the

presence of a dragon in these pages. What it was *not* designed to do is make you sick with horror and awe. So the snakelike head, the eyes with no pupils, the translucent wings—those were all left off.

You're welcome.

Gretel made a sign to the army. Arrows were notched. Bows began to bend.

The dragon disappeared from sight. Down below, all waited. Then it appeared again over the clearing—a little lower this time. It had seen the gold. It was circling. Gretel could hear her brother's breath coming quiet and quick. Hansel heard his sister's heartbeat mingling with his own.

The dragon flew over them again, lower, and was gone. Then again, lower still. Then again.

Gretel gestured at the sky. Arrows were aimed. They waited. The dragon flew over again. It was close enough that they could see the delicate scales of its skin gleaming in the moonlight, and its enormous, jagged talons. It flew over again, and this time the leaves on the trees shook from its passage.

The trees became still. They waited.

And waited.

No dragon.

Hansel and Gretel and all their soldiers stared up at the black, starry sky. Empty, save for the moon.

"What happened?" Gretel whispered to her brother. He shook his head and shrugged.

They waited longer. The people began to feel uneasy. They let their bowstrings go slack. They rubbed the sweaty handles of their weapons, trying to find a good purchase. Where, they wondered, was the dragon?

The darkness seemed to become heavier, more menacing. Glancing over their shoulders, they could see no more than a few feet into the forest.

Then, through the silence, there ran a sudden whisper in the leaves. The whole army stopped breathing all at once. They stood still and listened. Hansel felt something beneath his feet. Carefully, he lowered himself and put his hand on the earth. He felt it again.

"Gretel," he whispered. "The ground is shaking."

"I know," she whispered back. "I feel it."

It shook again. And again. Now all the men and women were looking frantically back and forth between the ground and the black forest that surrounded them.

People began to whisper. "What is it?" and "What's happening?"

"Shhh!" Gretel hissed. "Quiet!"

But they wouldn't quiet. They were afraid.

And then they saw it, weaving through the trees like an enormous snake with legs. Its wings were folded along its spine; its wide, viperlike head swung back and forth as it moved; and its golden eyes were shining in the moonlight.

It had come to take them from behind. And it was moving fast. So fast that the first villagers barely had time to scream before it was upon them.

Oh, I forgot to mention. The little kids? They *really* shouldn't be here for this.

Its mouth opened wide and snapped down on a woman with a bow. She hadn't even moved to defend herself. There hadn't been time. Now half of her was gone. Simultaneously, with a massive, taloned claw, the dragon swiped at a man with an ax. He landed on his back, ten feet away, without his internal organs.

With that, the forest awoke. Some of the people tried to fight the giant creature. Most tried to run. Occasionally, with a horrible, tearing sound, the dragon would kill someone else.

Hansel grabbed Gretel and held her tightly. "Don't go out there. It'll kill us. All of us." And then he called at the top of his lungs, "Retreat! Retreat! Retreat!"

The woods became madness. Screams rose and died. People ran in all directions. "Retreat!" Hansel shouted. "Retreat!"

"It's no good," Gretel said to him. "We've got to go."

"Where?" Hansel asked.

"To the dragon."

"What?"

"To lure it away. Run out ahead and make it chase us."

"It'll kill us," Hansel said.

Gretel set her mouth. "It's us or them."

Hansel took a deep breath. He nodded at Gretel. Then he stood up and made his way toward the sounds of death.

As he came near, he saw a man and a woman hiding behind a tree. The dragon was on the other side, its head moving this way and that, trying to see where they had gone. They had no weapons—they were shaking so badly they'd dropped them at their feet. Suddenly the dragon darted to one side of the tree. They froze.

Hansel cried out. The dragon turned in time to see Hansel scoop up a fallen spear and with one motion launch it the dragon's way. It glanced harmlessly off the dragon's black, snakelike scales. Hansel stopped. He stared.

Oh, he thought. And then he thought, *That's bad*.

Hansel spun to his left into the woods. The dragon followed.

"Get away!" Gretel bellowed at the remaining troops. "Get away!" And they did. They ran. On the ground were many bodies. But many more were now escaping through the dark underbrush.

The dragon was coming back. Gretel could hear it, feel it through the vibrations of the ground. She scrambled to hide. The dragon passed her, swift as water, its serpentine head swaying from side to side as it moved. From its mouth dripped blood. Suddenly, Gretel wondered what had happened to Hansel.

The dragon headed straight for the gold at the center of the clearing. Briefly, Gretel considered going to look for Hansel. But instead, making certain she wasn't seen or heard, Gretel followed the dragon's path. She crouched behind a thick thornbush at the clearing's edge. An ax lay not ten feet from her, out in the open. Gretel left it where it was.

The dragon was standing beside the cart of apples. It turned its head this way and that, and then began to pace, its golden eyes glaring at the glowing mountain.

Now the plan was working, Gretel realized, incredulous. The

dragon couldn't figure out how to take all the apples at once. It was confused. Frustrated. If only she still had an army to attack it.

After a few minutes, the dragon seemed to notice the other cart. It approached it and tore at the canvas with its teeth, revealing the barrels. It picked up one of the barrels with its massive jaws. It crushed it. Wine poured out—some down its throat, most onto the ground. The dragon spit out the staves of the broken barrel, shook itself, and resettled its wings on its back. It stood a moment, considering the stack of barrels. Then it took another in its mouth and drank it down just as it had the first one—but this time catching more of the wine in its throat.

It seemed to like it.

It did it again. And again. And again.

Gretel could not believe what she was seeing.

After the dragon had drunk six barrels of wine, it tried to rise into the air. But now its flight was wobbly and uncertain. *The dragon is drunk*, Gretel said to herself. She almost laughed.

The dragon came back to the ground and drank down four more barrels of wine. Soon it was teetering back and forth, even when it walked. It came up to the cart with the golden apples, stuck its head underneath, and tried to lift it.

Without a moment's hesitation, Gretel leaped from the thornbush and began to sprint toward the dragon. She could see its black leg, stuck out behind it, straining against the weight of the gold. She could see a thick pulsing vein running over the dragon's backward-bending knee joint. Gretel stooped for the ax without breaking her stride.

She covered the distance between the ax and the dragon quickly. She lifted the weapon high and brought it down.

The dragon screamed. It was a scream like nothing Gretel had ever heard before. She thought a hundred woodland creatures must all be dying at once—that was the sound. It pierced Gretel's head like a spear.

The dragon turned. It saw the little, golden-haired girl, holding an ax, frozen by the sound of its scream. It watched, shocked, drunken, disbelieving, as the little girl dropped the ax and sprinted off toward the woods. Behind her, on the ground, was an ax, covered in black dragon-blood. And two dragon toes.

The dragon shook itself, bellowed once, and followed, limping, after her.

Gretel heard the dragon coming. It sounded clumsy. Heavy. *The wine*, she thought. *And the toes, of course.* She cursed herself for missing the vein. She had never wielded an ax before.

Gretel wove through the trees, trying to keep ahead of it. Where was Hansel? What had happened to him? She could hear the dragon, wine-sodden and wounded as he was, catching up to her. *Just get away from it*, she thought. *Get free of it. So I can find Hansel, and we can get out of here.*

But how to get free of it? She thought of diving into a bush and letting the dragon run past. But it wouldn't run past. It would see her, and kill her. She thought of finding a narrow cave and crawling into it. Good idea, but where would she find a cave? And then, up ahead, she saw a tree. It was an enormous pine, easily the tallest tree in this part of the forest. Without thinking, without any plan at all, she made for it.

The pine's bristly branches started low to the ground and ran densely up the trunk. As soon as she arrived at its base, Gretel leaped onto the lowest ones and began to climb. She climbed around to the far side of the trunk, in the hope that the dragon might not see her.

When, a moment later, the dragon, drunk and limping, arrived at the tree's base, it was indeed confused. It seemed to know she had gotten up in the tree. But she was forty feet up by the time it realized she was on the other side of the trunk.

It set off after her. It tried to use its wings, but they would catch on the branches of the surrounding trees. It tried to climb, but the branches were too thin, and they went cracking and tumbling to the ground when it put its weight on them. So the dragon ended up digging its rough talons into the soft wood and ascending the trunk in leaps, smashing branches as it went.

The pine needles brushed at Gretel's face as she climbed, and the sticky sap of the tree stuck to her palms. Her heart was pounding from fatigue and fear. But there was no chance to rest. The dragon was gaining. Its leaps up the trunk gained it ten feet or more, while its occasional slides back down—stripping whatever branches it hadn't smashed on the way up—gained her only a few seconds at most. Her hand reached for the next branch and she pulled herself up. Her feet gained a secure hold and pushed her up to the next one. *Go*, she told herself. *Go*. And then she thought, *Where?* She looked up, hoping that perhaps the top of the tree would be too thin for the dragon to follow her onto. Perhaps it was. But it was also far above the other trees around it. Up there, the dragon could use its wings. *Just climb*, she told herself. *Just climb*. She reached up and grabbed onto the next branch.

"Wha—well, *excuse* us!" a voice said.

Gretel lost her grip and nearly fell out of the tree.

"Well, I never!" said the voice. "Some people!"

Gretel looked up. There was a thick mess of twigs and needles on the branch above her head.

"Well," said another voice, "see who it is!"

And then a black head, with black eyes and a black beak, peered over the branch above her.

"Well, I'll be!" said the first raven. "If it isn't Gretel!"

"No! Here?" said the second.

"Tell her to be more considerate of a raven's nest!" said the third. "Has she no manners? Was she raised by apes?"

"I think she was raised by a king and queen," said the second.

The ravens? In this *very* tree? Gretel could barely believe it. In fact, had it not been for all the strange, incredible things that had happened to her already, perhaps she wouldn't have. But after eating a house, and talking to the stars, and all the rest of it—well, she believed it just fine.

"Please!" she said. "Help me!"

The sound of tearing wood came from below. She looked down. The dragon had just slid halfway down the trunk again. "Please! There's a dragon after me!"

"Help you?" said the third raven. "After what you've done to our nest?"

"Oh, it's not so bad," said the second raven.

"You're not the one who's going to fix it, though, are you?" replied the third testily.

"I have my responsibilities, too. When food is scarce, and *my* job gets difficult, do I complain?" said the second raven.

"Yes," the other two ravens answered at once.

Below, the dragon regained his footing and was climbing again.

"Please!" Gretel cried.

"We can't help you," said the first.

"Yes," said the second. "It's not what we do."

Gretel looked down. The dragon was gaining quickly. She hadn't time to plead. "Then move!" she shouted, and clambered up onto their branch, just barely avoiding crushing their nest with her foot.

"Careful there!" the third raven cawed.

Gretel pushed past their branch, straining to keep ahead of the dragon. The first raven beat his wings beside her. "I'm sorry for my companion's rudeness," he said. "We understand the gravity of your situation." He looked down. "No pun intended, of course."

Gretel didn't know what he was talking about. "Are you going to help me or not?" she cried.

"I'm afraid we can't," the raven said. "You see, we can only *tell* the future. We can't attempt to change it. It wouldn't do any good, you see? It's the future."

There was an enormous crack from below, followed by terrible squawking. Gretel hurried her pace, but up ahead, the branches were thinning out to almost nothing. She was just about out of branches to climb to. And at any moment, the dragon would be able to fly. Just as Gretel realized there was nowhere else for her to go, around her head there was a frantic beating of wings and a very angry raven.

"Did you see that? Did you? Our nest! Gone! Crushed! Unbelievable! The height of inconsideration!"

The second raven fluttered up beside the third. "*Inconsiderateness*, I think, is the word."

"Either one is acceptable," said the first judiciously.

"I don't care about the stupid word!" the third raven cried. "I care about our nest!"

Suddenly, Gretel was nearly blown off the tree by a swift burst of air. She turned. The dragon was hovering beside her, beating its translucent wings, staring at her with its terrible golden eyes. The dragon's mouth was no more than six feet away. He opened it.

"Kill!" the third raven shrieked, and in one of the more comical acts of heroism Gretel had ever seen, the raven dove at the dragon's head. The dragon snapped at it, and the raven turned and headed back for the tree. "Retreat!" he cawed. "Temporary retreat!"

———

Now, the third raven was not afraid of dying. As the ravens have already implied, there are some things that they *do*, and some things they do not do. Dying is of the latter group.

Of course, getting trapped in the stomach of a dragon is, even for a creature that cannot die, an indescribably unpleasant experience.

Though not quite as unpleasant, I would imagine, as getting out again.

The dragon flew closer to Gretel. It snapped at her feet. Gretel could smell its hot horrible breath; see the blood and the foam mingling between its long, sharp teeth; hear the beating of its enormous heart out of time with the beat of its enormous wings. It lunged at her, not only with its head, but with its entire body. It knocked the branch she was standing on clear off the tree. She fell and grabbed hold of the only thing she could.

The dragon's neck.

The dragon reared backward. Perhaps if it had had its full wits about it, it might have managed to get her off its back. But as it was drunk, it circled in the air and snapped at its own shoulders, but could not manage to get her off.

"Attagirl!" cried the first raven.

"Yeehaw!" yelled the second.

"Incoming!" crowed the third, and it dove for the dragon's eyes. The dragon twisted away from the attack and beat its huge wings three or four times to rise above the tree. The ravens followed.

Up, up through the black, starry night they rose. Gretel held on tightly to the dragon's supple, scaly skin as its muscles rippled beneath her. Occasionally the dragon would twist to try to snap at her, but she was too close to its head. She worried that it might use its claws to get at her, as a dog gets at its fleas. But a dragon is not a dog, and that hadn't seemed to occur to it yet.

From time to time the ravens would reappear beside Gretel and make diving attacks at the dragon's eyes.

"Avenge the nest!" cried the third raven.

"A bird's nest is his castle!" cried the second, finally getting into it.

"Habeas corpus!" cried the first, somewhat tangentially.

So the dragon kept rising. The air became cold around Gretel's hands. Her knuckles turned blue. Soon, she and the dragon were higher than the ravens could fly. But the dragon didn't seem to mind. Its transparent wings took them higher and higher and higher still, until Gretel had to breathe hard to get any air at all, and her head began to spin. Still the dragon climbed.

And then Gretel heard a voice. It was low. And soft. And creepy. It said, "Fee-fie-foe-fesh, I think I smell child-flesh!"

Gretel looked up. There—very, very close—was the moon. His eyes were hard and glistening, like diamonds. His white lips were parted around his sharp, ivory teeth. He was watching Gretel as the dragon rose.

"Oh boy," Gretel muttered.

Snap! The cold breath of the moon froze the sweat on Gretel's neck. The dragon felt it, too, and turned. The moon snapped again. The dragon twisted. The moon wanted nothing to do with the dragon. Not that the moon is afraid of dragons. The moon is not afraid of anything, except the sun, and only then because the sun calls him names and he does not appreciate that. Still, the moon does not generally bother dragons. Of course, dragons do not often have children on their backs. And the moon rarely passes up an opportunity to taste the succulent, tender meat of a child.

The dragon twisted, and the moon snapped his teeth.

Twist!

Snap!

Twist!

Snap!

Twist!

Snap!

Gretel fumbled at her belt. She wanted to be eaten by the moon even less than by the dragon. She took out her little dagger. As the dragon twisted and the moon prepared to snap again, she plunged the dagger into the dragon's neck with all her might.

It did not pierce the scales, but the dragon turned toward her. And toward the moon.

It screamed.

Gretel fell through the air. Her arm was covered in black dragon-blood. Above her, the dragon was screaming its terrible scream and writhing back and forth. Above that, the moon was trying to spit the disgusting dragon-meat out of his mouth, and cursing himself for missing Gretel's tender flesh. She watched them disappear into the blackness as she fell.

Gretel would die any moment now. That was clear. She had been thousands of feet in the air. Higher than the ravens could fly. Soon she would hit the ground, and all of her bones would be broken, and her brain would smash through her skull, and her heart would stop beating immediately. Or, she thought, she would land on a sharp branch and be skewered like a piece of meat. Her speed increased as she fell. The cold air grew a little warmer. She could see the stars twinkling at her from above.

Then she hit something. It was soft, and she rolled off it and kept falling. She hit another soft thing, and then rolled off that. She hit a third soft thing, and then rolled off that and into the branches of a tree. She fell all the way down the tree, hitting its leafy branches as she fell. Then she hit the ground.

She was not dead.

She sat up and looked around. She was covered with black feathers. She heard a fluttering sound, and saw three woozy black ravens, missing most of their plumage, settling on a branch overhead.

"Ow," said the first raven.

"Ow," said the second raven.

"Ow," said the third raven.

"That hurt," they all said at once.

"You saved me!" Gretel said.

"Not intentionally," said the third raven.

"You just happened to hit us on your way down," said the second.

"Of course, we knew that would happen," said the first. "We just didn't know it would hurt so much."

Suddenly Gretel leaped to her feet and ran off into the woods.

"Manners!" said the third raven.

"We saved her life, and she just runs off without a thank-you?" said the second.

"She's going to find her brother," said the first.

"Oh yes," said the second.

"We knew that," said the third.

Gretel tore through the wood, branches slapping at her face, vines grabbing at her ankles. "Hansel!" she cried. "Hansel!" The creepy, child-eating moon shone down through the branches of the trees. She ran by his light.

Ahead, in the shadow of a pine sapling, lay a body. It was facedown on the ground. Gretel slowed and approached it. She turned it over and quickly turned away. It was not Hansel. It had a gash across its chest. And half a head. Gretel got up, swallowed bile, and began to run again.

She saw another body, lying half in a bush. She ran to it and pulled it out. A woman. Her chest was caved in, and her neck was bent at an unnatural angle. Gretel turned and ran on.

Bodies. More bodies. Gretel hadn't realized so many had fallen. There were dozens of them, scattered, lifeless, throughout the woods.

But where was Hansel? Where was he? Was he as lifeless as these bodies she found in the underbrush? Was he as still? As cold? Where was he?

Then the forest floor began to shine. White pebbles. The

white pebbles were lighting her way. She followed them. They brought her to the clearing.

There, standing at the clearing's center, was Hansel, covered in blood. She ran to him and threw her arms around him. "I'm okay," he said hoarsely. "It's not my blood. I was helping the wounded." She nodded and held him.

They followed the path of shining pebbles out of the woods. As they walked, the creepy moon illuminated the forest floor and the bodies scattered among the silent trees. Some faces were covered in blood, with eyes open but dead. Others were crushed beyond recognition. A hand was lodged in the crook of a branch. A young woman lay facedown, her hair spread out about her bloody head like a halo.

The children hid their faces.

Lost lives.

Empty bodies.

Hansel and Gretel held each other as they walked through the quiet, awful night.

Okay.

    Take a breath.

    Last story.

    Here we go.

HANSEL and GRETEL
and
Their Parents

*O*nce upon a time, two children, a boy named Hansel and a girl named Gretel, followed a path of shining pebbles out of a dark, bloody wood and into a small town. The inn of the town was lit, and the children could hear loud voices within. They walked to the door. They opened it. They were met with a roar.

"They live!" someone shouted, and they were swarmed by people, slapping their backs, rubbing their heads, embracing them.

"You did it!" they cried. "You survived!"

"And you saved us!" It was the man who had been hiding behind the tree. The woman was next to him. She beamed at them.

"Most of us," someone said. The cheers began to fade.

"And the dragon?" another asked. Now all became silent.

Hansel and Gretel stared at the people, their faces expectant, hopeful.

"It lives," Gretel said, shaking her head. "The dragon lives."

A long, heavy sigh passed through the room.

"We're sorry," Hansel said. "We tried."

"Oh, well that's good!" There was a young man sitting in the corner. He had a long fresh cut across his face that was yellow with balm. "The children tried! Well, that makes it all better!"

Hansel and Gretel stared at the young man and his grotesque, raw scar.

"They had a cute little idea," he went on, "and they gave it a shot! Good for you two!" His tone suddenly changed. "Do you know I nearly died out there? Do you know that we all nearly died!"

"We didn't, though," said a large man with a beard.

"*We* didn't. How many did? How many dead are there?"

There was silence. In their minds, Hansel and Gretel saw the bodies scattered among the trees. Gretel thought of the woman whose hair looked like a halo.

"They're children!" the scarred man shouted. "Children! We followed children to fight a dragon? What were we thinking?

What were any of us thinking?" He put his head in his arms on the table.

A woman nearby placed a hand on his shoulder. She glared at Hansel and Gretel.

The man with the beard stepped up to them. "Don't listen to them," he said. "You did good. Most of us lived. No one has ever survived a fight with the dragon before."

"And what's this on you?" said a woman, gesturing at Gretel. Gretel looked down. She was covered in the black blood of the dragon.

"We hurt it," Gretel said. "We took two of its toes and cut the side of its face." She did not explain that the moon had bitten half of its cheek off. She wasn't sure they would understand.

Her news was met with a louder roar than the one that had met them when they'd entered.

"Hurt it!" "Took two toes!" "Gashed its face!"

The bearded man squeezed each of their shoulders with a meaty hand. "You see? This was just the first battle. We'll get it next time. And now that we know we can beat it, you'll have a thousand more recruits. Ten thousand more!"

"And it will be a thousand times smarter!" the young man shouted from the corner. "And ten thousand times angrier! How many more people will die for this . . . this childishness? And now it will be worse than before. It will take revenge on all of us. On everyone."

There were scattered murmurs of agreement from around the tavern.

"What have we done?" he moaned.

Gretel's face was scorching. Hansel's lips were pressed together so hard they had turned white.

"There are dead in the forest," Hansel said at last.

"Yes," said the veteran. "We'll tend to them. You go home now."

The children turned and walked out of the tavern. As the door closed behind them, something hit it and clattered to the floor.

They walked back to the castle as the eastern horizon was just beginning to change from black to deep, deep blue. The moon had set. The air was cold and moist. After a while Gretel said, "It wasn't supposed to happen like that."

"So?" Hansel answered sullenly. "It did."

"But how?" Gretel replied, shaking her head. "It must have known somehow."

"Known what? What knew?"

"The dragon."

"What are you talking about?"

"It knew the plan. It saw the apples, and then it came through the woods to take us from behind."

"It didn't know," Hansel scoffed. He felt cold. He rubbed his arms up and down.

"It did. About everything except the wine." Gretel kicked the road. "Who knew our plan?"

"It didn't know," Hansel repeated. "Maybe it figured out the apples were a trap." His stomach twisted. "It was a stupid, childish plan."

"No," Gretel said. "No. It knew."

At the palace, the queen rushed up to them and took them in her arms. "Oh, my dears! You're safe! Oh, thank God you're safe!"

They told her what happened, and her face grew long and serious. "It isn't so bad. You wounded it. No one has ever done that before."

The children nodded.

"You did a very brave thing. Very brave." And she pulled them to her. When she released them, Hansel said, "Where's Father?"

"He locked himself in his room while you were gone," the queen replied. "He was so scared for you both that he was shaking. He said he tried to shave, but he cut himself. Quite seriously, it seems."

"Will he be okay?" Gretel asked.

"I'll be fine." Their father's voice echoed from across the hall. He limped toward them, a bandage wrapped around his head. He took them in his arms. "Foolish of me, shaving at a time like this. It calms me down when the barber does it. . . . But forget about your foolish father. You're all right?" He saw the dragon-blood on Gretel. "What happened to you? What is that stuff?"

So they all went and sat before the fire, and Hansel and Gretel told him about it, too. "You were very brave," he said when they'd finished. "And you nearly did a very great thing. You nearly saved this kingdom from the dragon."

"Nearly." Hansel and Gretel repeated the word together, and it stuck in their throats like a lump. Each saw, in their minds, the dead strewn across the forest floor.

At last, the king and queen took the children to bed, with Hansel helping his limping father up the stairs. Once in bed, their father kissed them both, and then their mother did, and then they closed the door and went away.

When their footsteps no longer sounded in the hall, Gretel sat up and opened the window curtains. The sun was beginning to come up. She opened the window and let the cool morning breeze blow in. She shook her head to get the terrible images of the night out of her mind. And the weight, the old weight, had returned.

"It knew," she said. "It knew our plan."

Hansel sat up. He felt the weight, too. Heavier than ever. As if every person in his family were standing on his chest. And every person in the Kingdom of Grimm on top of that. "Come off it," he said irritably. "It saw us, or heard us, or something. No one knew the plan until we were deep in the forest. And none of the soldiers ran off."

"Mother and Father knew it."

"Oh, please," Hansel said. "Mother and Father told the dragon?"

Gretel admitted that sounded ridiculous.

She sat, looking out the window. The kingdom spread out before her under the rising sun. Maybe the dragon had seen the golden apples and figured it out. It had been an obvious trap. A stupid trap. A childish trap.

But then . . .

"Why did Father have a bandage around his head?" Gretel asked suddenly.

"You heard. He cut himself."

Gretel nodded. After a moment, she said, "Why was he limping?"

"Because—" Hansel said, and then stopped.

"Was he shaving his toes?"

"Wait . . . I don't understand," said Hansel.

Gretel stood up. "Father," she said.

"What about him?" Hansel asked, staring.

"Father is the dragon."

"What?"

"When did the dragon first appear?" Gretel said. "When Father was away, looking for us. When did it kill the kingdom's army? When Father wasn't leading the army. Who knew of our plan? Mother and Father."

"But the wine—you said the dragon didn't know what was in those barrels."

Gretel paused, but then she replied, "When did we decide to bring the wine?"

"After we told them—"

"After we told them. And now he has a bandage on his head, and he's limping."

"No."

"It's him."

"He's our *father*."

"It doesn't matter," Gretel said. She went to the clothes she had worn for the battle, lying in a bloody pile on the floor, and drew from her belt the small dagger. She walked over to the door to the hall and opened it. She turned to Hansel. "I am going to kill the dragon."

Gretel walked slowly down the stairs and through the hall to their parents' room. She opened the door. The king stood in his nightclothes beside the bed. His foot was thickly bandaged, and blood was seeping through the wrappings.

"Where's Mother?" Gretel asked.

The king turned, surprised. "I thought you would be sleeping," he said. "She's in the chapel. Why?" And then, "Gretel, why do you have that dagger? What's wrong?"

"You are the dragon," she said.

"What?"

"You are the dragon!" she shouted. She took a step toward him. He took a step back. She stepped toward him again. Then she charged.

"Gretel!" he cried as she thrust the dagger at his chest. He stepped to the side and grabbed her arms. "Gretel! Stop! Stop! What are you doing?"

Just then, Hansel arrived at the door. He watched his father holding his sister's slender wrists with his strong hands. She was shouting at him, "You're the dragon! You're the dragon!"

and trying to hit him with the point of the dagger. He shook her—violently—and the dagger came loose from her hands. It clattered to the floor. He kicked it, and it slid under the bed.

He held her wrists tightly. "Gretel, what are you doing?"

Gretel's face was red and twisted with fury. "You did this to us!" she cried. "You cut off our heads! You're the dragon! You killed those people! It's your fault! Yours!" And she lifted her little foot and brought it down on his bandaged toes as hard as she could.

He threw his head back and screamed in pain.

She stomped on the bandage again and again. The bandage began to slide off. Still she stomped.

"Gretel!" Hansel shouted. "Stop! You're hurting him!"

But Gretel fell to the ground. "He's missing two toes!" she said. "He's missing two toes!"

Her father looked up at her. His eyes were not his eyes. They were golden, with neither whites nor pupils. "Hansel!" Gretel cried.

Hansel had seen. He was looking for a weapon. Hanging on the wall there was a sword. He took it down and moved toward his father—the dragon. His father stared at him through golden eyes. "I'm sorry, Father," Hansel whispered.

"It's not your fault," Gretel said.

And then Hansel's sword cut through the air toward their father's neck, and at that moment both Hansel and Gretel remembered just what it had looked like, just what it had felt like, when it had been them, not him. And then Hansel's sword took off their father's head at the neck and sent it rolling across the floor and into a corner of the room. The king's headless body fell on top of Gretel.

And just like that, everything was still.

Gretel cradled her father's body. Hansel's bloody sword tip touched the stone floor. The light in the room was yellow like the morning. The birds outside did not sing.

Then, out from where their father's head had once been attached to his body, two tiny claws emerged. They were quickly followed by spindly black legs, and then the golden eyes and head of a miniature, wormlike dragon. Its long, thin, black, blood-covered body slipped out of the king's neck and scrambled down his shoulder, and, before she could even move, over Gretel's lap and onto the floor. It skittered frantically toward the sewage grate, its claws scratching and scraping against the bedroom's flagstones.

Gretel shrieked and Hansel flung himself at it, striking at its skeletal body with his sword. One furious blow broke its back. The next decapitated it completely. But Hansel didn't stop. He raised his sword and brought it down again and again and again, until the evil little creature was nothing more than a mess of black, pulpy pieces on the floor. Hansel, breathing hard, eyes aflame, took the ash shovel from the fireplace. He collected the tiny beast's mangled remains and threw them into the fire. The flames roared in greeting, and as they did a long, high, terrible scream pierced the air—just like the screams Hansel and Gretel had heard in the woods.

A moment later, all was silence again, and golden smoke drifted lazily from the blazing fire into the chimney, and then out onto the morning air.

The dragon was dead.

Hansel looked to Gretel. She sat, bent over her father's lifeless body. She was crying. Hansel came to her side and hugged her. And Hansel and Gretel, brother and sister, sat on the floor of their parents' room and thought of all they had seen, and all they had done. And they wept.

The End

Almost.

"Quick," Gretel whispered through her tears. "Bring me his head."

Hansel looked to the corner where it had come to rest. He went to it and—gingerly, trying not to look—he picked it up. Then he brought it to his sister.

From her pocket Gretel had taken out the warlock's twine. It was nearly nothing. Just a frayed strand, no thicker than a hair.

"Hold his head on," she said.

So Hansel put their father's head on his neck. Then Gretel wrapped the twine around it and, fumblingly, tied it. As she untied it, the twine snapped. She let it fall to the ground.

They watched the skin on their father's neck creep together, healing before their eyes. But he did not move.

Gretel began to cry harder. Hansel cried, too.

"We forgive you," Gretel said.

"We do," Hansel agreed. Their tears fell on him.

And he moved. Gretel nearly threw him off her, she was so surprised. The king groaned.

"Father? Father!" Gretel cried. He groaned again. His eyes opened slowly.

"Hello," he said.

Hansel and Gretel fell upon him. "Oh, Father, you're all right! You're all right!"

Gretel said, "We wish we hadn't had to do that."

Hansel said, "But we did have to."

He took hold of them both. "I understand," he said. And then, blinking at them as if he had just walked into the sunlight after a long time in the darkness, he said, "I under-stand, my children."

Just then they heard footsteps in the hall. The queen's. Hansel looked at his father, covered in blood.

"Father," he said, "did Mother know you were the dragon?"

"No," their father replied. "I didn't know myself, until just now. I just kept waking up in strange places. I really did think I was shav—"

"Okay. Get in the wardrobe." So their father got in the wardrobe. Just as he did, their mother entered the room.

"Did you have a nice time praying, Mother?" Hansel asked.

She took her children in her arms. "Oh, I can barely pray. I think only of the dragon, and of our poor kingdom."

Gretel said, "What if we told you, Mother, that we knew who the dragon was, and that the only way to stop the dragon would be to kill that person?"

The queen looked back and forth between her two children. "You know who it is? Then we must do it! Right away!"

"No matter who it is?" Hansel asked.

"No matter who it is."

"It's Father," the children said at once.

The queen gasped. She fell to the floor and wept bitterly.

After a long time, she said, "If you're sure it's him, if you can prove it—then yes. I couldn't do it. But I would understand."

The children looked at each other, and then said, at the same moment, "Are we glad you said that!" Then they walked over to the wardrobe and let out their father, all covered in blood.

The queen screamed. Then Hansel and Gretel explained it all. The queen wept and beat the king's chest with her hands. But after that she laughed through her tears and threw her arms around all of them. Then she wept some more.

"You're all okay?" she asked, as tears streamed down her face.

"We're all okay," they said together.

And they all held one another—one big, happy, sad, complicated family—as tightly as they always should have.

The End

Nearly.

I'm sorry. Before I tell you the very, truly, absolutely end, I've got to interject one last time.

For fun.

Or to help you, if I can. (Though I wouldn't count on it.)

Why did this patricidal beheading have to happen? Why something so awful? So gruesome? So upsetting? Why was their father the dragon? And did they really, really have to cut off his head?

And what about everything that came before that? All this blood and this pain. What sense does any of it make? Is there any sense at all?

I don't know.

I mean, what does under-standing have to do with returning to your family? Or cutting off your finger have to do with turning into a wild beast? What does an old crone with a shackle on her leg have to do with Faithful Johannes? Or three black ravens with cages full of white doves? Why is the moon creepy and cold, when the stars are bright and kind? Why was the widow a good parent, and yet no more able to protect Gretel than the bad parents? What did all of this mean—these strange, scary, dark, grim tales?

I told you already. I don't know.

Besides, even if I did, I wouldn't tell you.

You see, to find the brightest wisdom one must pass through the darkest zones. And through the darkest zones there can be no guide.

No guide, that is, but courage.

As Hansel and Gretel and the queen and king held one other, the final golden fumes of the dragon drifted from the chimney and out onto the morning air. The gold mingled with the sunrise and slowly suffused itself over the whole kingdom. As people woke that morning, they saw it. They were drawn out of their houses by it, by the beautifully golden smoke that floated beneath the clouds. They followed it. Without wondering, without saying a word, they followed it. As if they knew, upon seeing it, that something had happened. Something important. And that, to find out what it was, all they had to do was follow the golden smoke.

Along the roads, the subjects of Grimm walked silently toward the source of the beautiful golden light. Toward the castle.

———

"You never told us," the queen said to her children as they sat on the floor of the bedroom, blood winding through the crevices of the stones, collecting in little pools. "You never told us where you've been, and what you've done."

Hansel and Gretel looked at each other.

"You don't have to tell us," their father said gently. "Not now. Not ever if you don't want to."

Hansel held his sister in his gaze. Her eyes, ocean-blue, sun-bright, were happier, clearer than he had seen them in a long, long time. Gretel returned her brother's stare. He looked unburdened. Lighter. And he looked older than he had ever looked. Not old with care. Old with wisdom.

"We can tell you now," Gretel said.

And so they did. Hansel started with what Johannes had told him, about the old king, lying on his deathbed. Gretel planned to pick up as soon as she and Hansel entered the story.

But just then there was a knock on the king and queen's chamber door.

"Yes?" said the king.

A servant poked his head in. "Excuse me, Your Majesty," he said. Then he saw blood on the king. "Your Majesty! Are you all right?"

"I'm fine," said the king. "What is it?"

"I . . . uh . . ." The servant, named Wilhelm, shook his head and tried not to stare at the blood. "Your people," he went on. "They're standing outside the castle."

"What? What people?"

"The subjects."

"Which subjects?" the queen demanded.

"All of them, Your Majesties."

The king and queen leaped to their feet. "But why?" the queen asked.

"I . . . I'm not sure," said the servant. "I think it might have to do with the golden smoke."

"What smoke?" said the queen.

"The dragon," Gretel whispered to her.

"What?" the king said. Hansel gave him a meaningful look. "Oh," he said. "Right." He turned to his wife. "Should we go down?" He looked concerned.

The queen looked at her children.

"It's okay," Hansel said. Gretel nodded.

But the queen said, "No. Let them wait."

"But, Your Majesty!" the servant said. "They're calling for you!"

"Let them call," the queen replied.

The king added, "Try to keep them entertained."

The servant was about to protest again, but, on seeing the expressions on his masters' faces, thought better of it. He closed the door. Hansel and Gretel smiled at their parents, and Hansel started again.

In the hallway, the other servants crowded around Wilhelm. "What are we supposed to do?" one asked.

"Keep them entertained," Wilhelm said. "Somehow."

"What are they saying in there?" another asked. "I think I hear the children talking."

So the servants leaned their heads against the door. Hansel was telling of the portrait of the golden princess.

"Quick!" said Wilhelm. "Go get everyone you can. Every servant in the castle." So one of them did, as the others continued to listen at the door.

When all the servants were assembled, Wilhelm said, "Jacob and I"—he gestured to the servant to his right—"are going to listen at the door and relay everything we hear. Then you pass it down, as best you can, to the next servant, and keep passing it, all the way out to the balcony. The royal crier will stand on the balcony and relay it all to the subjects." He turned to the kitchen staff. "Go and make food. For everybody."

"For everybody?!" the chief cook exclaimed.

"Everybody!"

And so the plan was carried out. Hansel and Gretel told the whole tale, from the old king's deathbed all the way through the beheading of their father. And the servants relayed it, as best as they could, down the halls of the castle and out to the royal crier, who in turn relayed it to the people of the Kingdom of Grimm.

The storytelling took all through the day, and into the early evening. And then, as the stars were beginning to twinkle, but before the creepy moon had made an appearance in the southern sky, Hansel and Gretel finished. The family hugged one another once more, very tightly, and stood up. They stretched their arms and legs, and then they went to the door. The servants had retreated to the opposite wall of the corridor. When the king came out, he asked what they were all doing there. Wilhelm said that they were ready to take them down to the great balcony, where their subjects were still waiting. They'd been fed.

"You fed them?" the queen said. "That was very clever of you."

Wilhelm bowed.

"What did you tell them?" the king asked.

Wilhelm rubbed his hand nervously over his hair. He looked at Jacob and the other servants. They all looked at the floor. He said, "We told them what Hansel and Gretel told you. About their adventures." The queen raised her eyebrows. "And let me be the first to congratulate the children," he added quickly, "on the successful vanquishing of the dragon. We are all more grateful than words can express." And he said it like he meant it.

The queen looked at the king, but the king only smiled. "Fine," he said. "Well done. That's fine." He, too, said it like he meant it. Then the royal family followed the line of servants down to the balcony.

The subjects of the Kingdom of Grimm were spread out before the balcony in the thousands, sitting on the ground, eating the suppers that the kitchen had provided them, and listening to the end of the story with rapt attention.

"I understand," the crier was saying as the king and queen and Hansel and Gretel emerged from behind him. "I understand, my children."

A roar erupted from the subjects. The crier, thinking they were roaring for his telling of the story, took a little bow. But then he saw the royal family. Quickly, he retreated.

The subjects' cheers were deafening. Hansel and Gretel stood before them and took it all in. They smiled.

Then the king raised his hands. The subjects quickly grew quiet.

"I have something I must say," he announced. "These two children have killed the dragon. Killed the dragon, when everyone else had tried, and everyone else had failed."

The subjects cheered wildly. The king raised his hands again for silence.

"The dragon would have destroyed this kingdom altogether," he went on. "It would have left it an empty ruin." He paused. He tried to swallow down a thickness that had developed in his throat. "*I* would have left it an empty ruin. I didn't know what I was doing, of course. I did not know I was the dragon. But the dragon, I, would have destroyed this kingdom if Hansel and Gretel had not stopped me."

The people of Grimm stared.

"I can no longer be king. How could I? After what I have done?"

In all the Kingdom of Grimm, not a single person made a single sound.

"I am passing my crown on. And I ask my wife to do the same. We will pass our crowns to our children."

A murmur swept through the crowd. "To Hansel and Gretel? To children?"

ADAM GIDWITZ

"Yes!" the king declared. "They are children. But they are the wisest, bravest children I have ever known. My wife and I will help them as long as they need us to. But"—and here he held up his hand, and all murmuring stopped—"there is a wisdom in children, a kind of knowing, a kind of believing, that we, as adults, do not have. There is a time when a kingdom needs its children. These children. King Hansel and Queen Gretel."

Total silence.

"They will, of course, marry other people," the queen added.

Still, total silence.

And then, in the crowd, the tall man from Wachsend, the bald one with the boxer's nose, shouted out, "But they're just little ki—"

But before he could finish, someone else called out. It was a young man with long hair and a fresh, raw scar on his face. The one from the tavern. He had climbed up on the shoulders of a friend. Hansel and Gretel saw him. His face was shining. "They saved us from the dragon!" he cried. "Long live King Hansel! Long live Queen Gretel!"

The people of Grimm gazed up at Hansel and Gretel. There was something in what the king had said. About children. About these children.

"Long live King Hansel!" the young man shouted again. And then someone else took up the cheer. "Long live Queen Gretel!"

Another cried it. And another. More and more, more and more, rising up in a tumult all around Hansel and Gretel. "Long live King Hansel! Long live Queen Gretel!"

As they looked out over the people of Grimm, their father leaned down to them and said, "These subjects are your children now."

And their mother said, "You must take care of them."

"Better," their father added, "than we took care of you."

Hansel turned to him, and, smiling, gesturing at the crowd, said, "It looks like you did all right." Gretel reached out and took her father's hand, and then her mother's.

The subjects continued to cheer, till their throats strained and the sky seemed to whirl. "Long live King Hansel!" they cried. "Long live Queen Gretel! Long live Hansel and Gretel!"

And you know what?

They did.

ADAM GIDWITZ

Really.

Acknowledgments

Once upon a time, there was a brilliant woman named Gabrielle Howard, who wasn't very tall, and had a lovely English accent, and who was the lower-school principal at Saint Ann's School, in Brooklyn, New York. One fine day, Gabe, as she's called, came into my second-grade classroom and read Grimm's *The Seven Ravens* to my students (you now know, dear reader, that the Brothers Grimm should have called it *The Seven Swallows*—just another one of their many, many errors). As you also now know, the little girl in *The Seven Swallows* cuts off her finger. So after Gabe had finished reading the story, and after I had been resuscitated with a defibrillator, and after Gabe had assured me that I was not fired, because, after all, *she* had read the story to the students, and not me, I decided that there was something to these Grimm tales, and that I really should look into them. So it was Gabe Howard who introduced me to Grimm, and Gabe Howard who taught me, and still does teach me, to trust that children can handle it. No matter what "it" is. (Once, she proposed I stage *King Lear* with a class of second graders. We, led by the brilliant Sarah Phipps, did *Twelfth Night* instead.)

The students at Saint Ann's are my muses. It was, in fact, a class of first graders who insisted I tell them story after story after story, and thereby suggested to me that I had stories that kids wanted to hear. It is my students' thirst for understanding, their questioning, their calling-out, their thinking, their art, their calling-out-some-more, their writing, their still-calling-out-even-though-I-am-standing-right-in-front-of-them-asking-them-to-stop, and, above all, their growing that inspire me.

I must thank my teachers from The Park School of Baltimore. I think about all of them, every single day. I really do. One of them, Laura Amy Schlitz, read the English version of A *Smile as Red as Blood* to me when I was very young, thus warping my mind forever. She still teaches me and inspires me and has kept my spirits up as I traveled through this dark tale.

I have done nothing in the realm of writing and trying to publish my writing without consulting Sarah Burnes, who has been right about just about everything she has ever said to me. She identified me as a writer before I did, and then she told me what in my writing was good and what was bad until we got to where we are. Among her most brilliant acts of guidance was introducing me to Julie Strauss-Gabel. Before she met me, Julie believed that she knew the true story of Hansel and Gretel. But, together, we figured out what the real story was. She has been as much a partner as an editor, and there is no question that I would have produced the wrong, fake, untrue story of Hansel and Gretel had it not been for her.

Some dear friends and family members have read this book and given me invaluable ideas and criticism: John, Patricia, and Zachary Gidwitz; Adele Gidwitz (my first reader); Erica Hickey; and Lauren Mancia.

Indeed, Lauren Mancia has been there for every good and bad idea I have had about anything for the last seven years. And I hope for the next seventy.

Finally, I must acknowledge the Brothers Grimm. It

was they who wrote down these dark, grim tales, and it was their vision and voice that inspired this book. If you haven't read their versions of the tales, you must. Their impact on me, and on all of us, has been immeasurable.

Also, their stories are awesome.